BUG BOY

BY
EVER WALKER

Chapter 1

THE TERRIBLE SANDS

As I wait for Her, I curse the day I laid eyes on those terrible sands. And the bugs they gave to me.

The Bugs. I feel them now working their way underneath my skin. Oh, I pray for them to crawl out of me. Blind me! Burst my eyeballs in a bloody flight. I don't care. If only to relieve my pain for a brief moment.

Even with my bones brittle to their core and my skin sagging and rotten, they push me on, making me shuffle along with my mouth closed and my head down.

How I used to laugh at those afflicted like me! The walking dead I called them.

But I didn't know. How could I?

I can only wait for the peace promised by "She Who Shall Not Be Named." A serenity I cannot wait for.

Besides, who am I kidding? I couldn't kill myself if I wanted to. They won't let me.

Although this is the fault of Joy and John, I refuse to blame them. For their fate was a million times worse than mine. And they were the closest things to friends I have ever known.

John's thirst for adventure started all of this. How we laughed and acted like a couple of idiots back then. That laughter still echoes in my ears. Even now, it mocks me.

John showed me a picture of a rock he'd found online. It was a simple piece of lava with an image carved on its surface.

I told John it could be anything. Maybe some weird polarity in prehistoric times caused the lava to flow that way. But one look at it, and you knew. You knew some cruel appendage carved it long ago.

They'd found it after a tsunami disaster in Japan. All manner of odd things from the deep ocean washed ashore that day. Exotic fish no one knew existed, dark ocean plants; even old boats sunk long ago came up from the depths and landed miles inland.

Scientists stated this particular rock came from the bottom of the ocean, from the deepest part of the underwater universe. They believed it dated to several million years ago, yet on its surface was a picture of a face.

Such a hideous visage. Even through the blurred pixels of the online picture, I felt its eyes stare into my soul.

Little did anyone know or suspect at the time, but this rock was the harbinger for the end of the world. A message we didn't deserve.

And a message we didn't heed.

Chapter 2

JOHN O'CONNELL

John and I made the perfect roommates in college. I liked to pass gas – and he liked to punch people who passed gas in the balls.

Our university was in Southern California. We both came from different parts of the country, but people still thought we were locals. Tall, bulky and tanned. We fit right in.

We didn't sit still for a moment. Both of us wanted to prove something to the world,. and we stepped on anyone or anything which stood in the way of our ambitions.

Sure, we were bullies. But we also knew how to kiss ass. As long as we garnered success, who cared about the consequences – or even the humiliation?

We both joined a fraternity. John wanted us to. We needed to network, get drunk and make out with ladies. The hazing was the only hard part.

For months – maybe as much as a year – they did all manner of cruel things to both John and me. They took us to remote places. Tied us up. Shoved rocks and twigs down our throats and up our butts.

I was good with all of it, except for the "cage." On weekends, they put rushes into the cage at random, for hours at a time. One weekend, they locked me in and forgot about me.

For the first six hours, I was okay. And then I started thinking about my assignments, my teachers and my student loans. With the cage so small, standing up was impossible. I freaked out.

When they did remember to check on me the following day, they found the cage turned over and a bloody mess inside. Those cages are sturdier than people realize.

Needless to say, when our turn came to haze the new rushes, we loved it. Waking them up in the middle of the night to throw them naked into the ladies' dormitory or taping them to a chair before their final was a blast.

One thing I must mention. Unlike the other jerks in our house, I did not lack compassion.

One time, when we hazed some freshman, we took them to a football field and started tackling them. One boy in particular was too frail for us. There was no chance we would take him into our house. After being tackled, he fell backward with his arm underneath him. He screamed and cried but they kept hitting him. Seeing enough, I stepped in and made them stop. After picking the boy up, I took him home. Later, I paid a price for it. My brothers put me in a sack and threw me in a pool.

I never regretted it.

John, on the other hand, was more political than me. He didn't put his neck out for anyone, let alone some skinny stupid kid who wanted to be bullied. Still, he was a good friend. He always had my back with the other fraters.

At one of our skull and bones ceremonies, John stood up for me. These ceremonies were our most formal of gatherings. We wore dark robes. Turned off the lights. Lit a candle on a plastic skull placed atop a fold-out, aluminum table, and sat with our arms crossed on orange chairs we stole from a classroom.

The Hypophetes brought up how some of the seniors didn't like me. When he asked the group about this, they all stomped their feet in response. Then, one of the elders stood up and accused me of being a dick.

When he asked someone to vouch for me, John stood up with his hands on his hips, looked around the room and said, "I will."

My mother raised me by herself in a small single-family house. My father left us just after I was born, never lending us any kind of financial support. A male friend from a stable background who wanted to help me gave me hope. Even if John was a narcissistic twat, he still fit the bill.

The Hypophetes asked, "What will you say?"

After looking around the room again, he said one word. "Bullshit."

At this, the entire room broke out in a round of stomping lasting several minutes and led to them adjourning the meeting and all of us getting drunk. I was saved.

As much as I looked up to John, he was flawed. He resented people for no reason. He hated those he deemed weak or weird. Being a friend of outstanding moral character, I would egg him on. One time, I almost helped him get expelled.

Sitting in the student commons, John convinced himself that some guy sitting next to the water fountain looked at him funny. This guy was geeky looking with glasses, black clothes and poor hygiene. I said, "Yeah, John, when we walked in, I saw him laughing at you."

John said, "Bastard. Just look at that loser."

I said, "You can't let him get away with that. Do something about it."

He said, "Hell yeah, I will."

And, after saying that, he walked over and kicked the poor guy right into the fountain. Too bad for John, half of the university watched him do it, including a few security guards. They escorted John out. I didn't see him again until that night.

He told me that he went to see the Dean. The Dean had recommended anger management classes for him. Which was really funny since he was an angry guy.

I loved hanging out with John in college and causing problems for other people. Unfortunately, our relationship hit an unexpected roadblock.

He found a girlfriend.

Chapter 3

JOY ROBERTSON

Joy was small and pretty, but her cute demeanor hid a powerful physical frame and a real bitch. You didn't want to cross her. Of all the crap I liked to be messed with on a daily basis, she was last on my list.

One day, when John wasn't around, she was at our house. I'd been drinking, and I bumped into her from behind. Without saying a word, she turned around and punched me with her phone. I think she meant to hit me in the chest, but she caught me square in the throat. I fell to my knees gasping for air.

Without missing a beat, she leaned forward and whispered into my ear, "Listen, Bastard, John and I have a good thing going. Unlike you, he has a future. So don't screw it up. Or I will screw you up."

Once, John told me her background. Evidently, to help pay for college, she'd worked in a cannery during high school and learned how to defend herself from drunk fishermen twice her age.

For the most part, she was cool. Like John, she watched out for people in her circle, even me. Still, I considered her highly strung.

In less than a second, she went from pure joy to unstoppable anger. She saw an order to everything. If someone violated this order, watch out. In such situations, she pursued a scorched-earth policy. Joy not getting her way was akin to opening the seventh gate of hell. At first, you felt something unsettling in the air, and then it became like the apocalypse.

Even the drink cups at a holiday party struck fear into all of us. If you opted for a larger cup and shunned the smaller, more stylish cups she'd planned her party with, the whole event was ruined. Actually, it jeopardized existence as we knew it. And, until everyone lined up to apologize to her for one man's large cup transgression, the restoration of life's balance was in doubt.

Personally, I thought she would be the next axe murderer in our city. An early, bloody death for John was his likely fate. But John didn't see it that way. He saw Joy as someone who added stability to his life and kept his emotions in check. And, with her around, it kept me and his other fraters from using him as a sucker.

Joy worked hard too. In addition to college, she worked several jobs, rising to management status in most of them. Granted, these jobs were in retail and hospitality. Still, the idea of John and me becoming managers was far-fetched. If anything, our qualifications limited us to dishwashers and bussers.

So, it shocked me to find out she supported him in his adventures. True, these trips took place over the summer and his father financed them. Still, it required the three of us traveling to unknown regions on a whim. Sometimes, John might ask us to go to San Francisco to hang out and drink coffee with him for a week; another, to Santa Barbara to check out the surf and ice cream.

I doubted Joy had ever been to any of these places. And her agreeing to come along always shocked me. Looking back on it now, I believe she went along to keep John close by, despite the stress it caused her to reschedule her job and classes.

Nevertheless, there is one thing I know for certain: None of us foresaw John's travels leading to a painful death for all of us.

Chapter 4

IMAGE ON THE INTERNET

Everyone witnessed the tragedy. An earthquake off the coast of Northern Japan and the subsequent tidal wave which engulfed the entire town. Equal parts humanity and terror. It was horrible to watch.

When the waters receded, we thought it had ended. However, the seas revealed even more horrors from its depths. For weeks after, we witnessed videos of dark things jumping about the ruins of the lost town. And strange objects lying in the mud left by the retreating waters.

Some saw this as the end of the world. They believed the earth revolted against the cancer of humanity which had poisoned the planet. Personally, I believed they looked too much into the disaster. And, in retrospect, they were a little wrong. It wasn't just this planet that hated us but the entire universe.

An image on the internet from the tragedy had caught John's attention. Actually, it became his obsession. Carved on a piece of lava rock. It portrayed what looked like the face of an insect with large hate-filled, human eyes.

Scientists believed this rock was millions of years old. Everyone laughed at them. I found it easy to criticize them as well, since I lacked the mental fortitude to conceive of a historical time frame beyond that of the past two thousand years.

Most rational people thought the scientists were pandering for research dollars, but not John. He even looked for someone at college who could translate their findings.

A young Japanese brother in our house named Yukio ended up helping him. Yukio was infamous for being able to take abuse. No matter what kind of new tortures we thought up, he greeted them with the same apathetic frown and look in his eyes. God created him for the sole purpose of joining a fraternity.

Yukio said the researchers were most interested in what was used to carve the rock. They figured that if they could determine the implement, then they could determine how they carved it. Maybe some weird polarity in the lava flow had caused it – or even a water current bumping it against other rocks.

What they discovered horrified them and made them an even greater source of ridicule for the simple minded like me. They said that not only was a hand tool used on the rock when it was still soft, but that something carved it with great attention to detail. For the lines were uniform and accurate. And drawn with equal depth.

Upon hearing this, John became convinced that there must exist some precedence for the carving. Surely, someone made a record of it before, during the course of human history.

He went to libraries and poured through publications that weren't on the internet. For months, he went to libraries all over Los Angeles. And then, one day, he hit pay dirt. In an arts and crafts magazine published in the 1970s, he found a similar image. Although the publication didn't note the location of the picture, it did list its photographer as living in New Mexico.

John contacted the photographer and asked her about the picture. She said that she took the picture at a town located off the main highway between Albuquerque and Santa Fe, during a festival. She thought it was a green chili festival.

Hearing this, John wanted to go there right away. He started talking to Joy and me about New Mexico festivals and how great the green chilies were.

I said, "Hey, man, what's the point of finding that thing, anyway? It exists, so what?"

John said, "Nah, you don't get it. We find that thing and we become an internet sensation. We find anything like the one in Japan, and we could be millionaires."

I said, "Yeah, but your dad's already rich."

He said, "But you aren't."

I said, "Good point."

Honestly, I didn't think for a second that John did this for me. And, it goes without saying, if we did benefit from going there in any way, John planned on taking all of it. Still, New Mexico was some place new for us – and John said he would pay for it. So, I went along.

John convinced Joy to take some time off from work as well. She didn't like it. She hated taking breaks from work. But, after some coaxing, she came along.

I say "coaxing," but all John needed to do was say my name. She wanted to come along just to keep an eye on the two of us.

Sadly, when we put one foot on the plane to Albuquerque, we took the first step to our mutual demise. All we'd accomplished together – all of our memories – became nothing more than trash at that moment.

And we did so with joy in our hearts.

Chapter 5

LAND OF ENCHANTMENT

On our approach to Albuquerque, I felt right away something was wrong. An updraft sent us into turbulence, causing the entire plane to shake from fore to aft for several minutes. Oddly, no one panicked. Everyone in our cabin remained silent, as if they accepted their fate.

Once we started our descent, the plane fell at a sharp angle. Either helped by the winds or the pilot's steering, we headed straight downward. As the airport came into focus, I saw a gloom all around us, although the sun was high in the sky. I wondered, was Albuquerque one of the gates of hell?

I said, "Man, this is a messed-up place."

John heard me but didn't look my way. He was scared shitless. Joy looked asleep with her head against the window. I'd picked a couple of real winners as friends.

As the plane's wheels hit the ground, the plane bounced. When we came back down to the tarmac, the pilot hit the brakes and pushed the passengers forward, moments after their heads almost hit the plane's roof. As I landed back into my seat, my chin came within inches of the headrest in front of me.

I said, "Either the pilots really suck at their jobs, or they are sadists."

Joy let me know she was awake. She said, "Shut the hell up."

After we taxied to the gate area, the baggage handlers brought metal steps for us to disembark with, instead of allowing the plane to pull all the way to the gate.

I thought to myself, *What a bunch of dicks. They won't even let us unload inside the terminal.*

Walking across the tarmac to the lower level and the baggage claim inside, everyone around us had sullen faces and slumped shoulders. Up to now, I didn't spend a lot of time in airports. Still, it seemed too quiet.

From the baggage claim, we took a shuttle to our rental car. Thank God John had decided on an SUV. I felt cramped enough on our flight from hell.

John set us up overnight in a two-bed hotel room. He planned on seeing the photographer first thing in the morning prior to heading out of the city.

That night, we went to a bar for some food since nothing else was open. The place was bizarre and had red leather seats, no windows and a one-entree menu listed on a chalkboard over the bar. The place felt out of time. It belonged back in the Route 66 days.

Something that needs saying about the Land of Enchantment, is that there's is a general unease about the place. Its history is the root of the cause. Once you understand New Mexico's history, you can accept its hellish nature. For it's a much older and brutal place than most people realize.

Before the colonies, conflict and strife raged here. The people who owned this land fought between themselves and with several races and religions for hundreds of years. The conquered and subjugated built the few buildings which remain. Admiring these buildings for their historical significance misses the whole point of their existence. If anything, wise people fear them.

When we woke the next morning, we grabbed a few coffees and hit the road. The photographer was not far from the hotel. And the more we moved, the less flight lethargy we felt.

The photographer lived in a small apartment on one of the larger boulevards. By larger, I mean, she was next to a strip mall with a few fast-food places.

When we exited the truck, John said, "Let me ask the questions. She likes to talk, but. I don't want to spend too much time here."

Going up a few flights of steps, we spotted her door right away. It was the only one with a picture on it. All the other doors were bare, except for hers. On her door, she'd painted a large cartoon caricature of a poodle.

John knocked.

We heard a woman say, "Hello?"

John answered, "Hi, it's John. We talked on the phone."

We heard a few dull thuds on the floor and then the door opened. In front of us stood a little old lady with a cane.

She said, "Hello, please come on in."

All sorts of knick-knacks, souvenirs and posters covered her apartment. And, of course, she owned a poodle.

After we sat down on a pink, microfiber couch, John said, "Thank you for meeting with us. We won't take much of your time. We just want to talk to you about the pictures I emailed. The ones I think you took."

When John copied the pictures of the magazine, he'd kept them on his phone. He avoided showing them to people because he didn't want to jeopardize his "investigation". He was a real columbo.

She said, "Yes, it's been so long since I saw those. I found more pictures I took from that day if you want to see them?"

An excited grin spread across John's face. "Yes, that would be great!"

The photographer picked up a large folder in front of her from the coffee table and handed it to John. Judging by the weight of the folder and how the photographer used both hands to lift it, I knew this would take longer than John had planned.

I said, "Can I use your bathroom?"

When she said yes, I went and sat on the toilet with the lid down so I could surf the web on my phone. I noticed that her bathroom walls held disability aides: bars. Her condition was clearly long term.

After half an hour, I grew bored and went back to the living room. From behind the couch, I heard multiple conversations. John talking to himself; and Joy talking to the photographer. It sounded like a real good party minus any fun.

I sat back down. "So, what did we find out?"

John said, "Well, good news and bad news."

I said, "Yes?"

He said, "The images in the pictures we have are from souvenirs, not from any old stones. But we know the place that sells the souvenirs."

Turning to the lady, he said, "Can you tell me again where you took these pictures?"

She screwed up her face. "But I really want to forget that place."

John asked, "Why's that?"

She said, "That's where I got my infection."

John said, "Infection?"

Evidently, after visiting the town in question, she'd woken up with four, thimble-sized holes in the back of her leg. At first, the holes were not painful. Just her leg behaved strangely. She found it difficult to use. Her leg behaved almost like it had a life of its own.

However, within a week, her leg started to smell. And it hurt so much, she made her neighbor take her to the hospital. At the hospital, the doctor advised amputation, since gangrene had set in.

After her amputation, they took a biopsy and examined the leg in full. They found two significant items of note. One, even though her leg had died at the outset of the infection, it still walked. And two, inside her bones, in tiny little elliptical holes, they found what looked like insect larvae.

Gross.

Hearing this sent my trypophobia into overdrive. I felt my jaw lock and my face lose its color. I even tasted something metallic in my mouth.

I said, "Jesus Christ."

John gave me a hard glance.

I said, "What?"

He turned to the photographer. "That's terrible. Did they ever find out what caused it?"

She said, "No, they didn't. But I never went back to that town. I didn't want to lose another leg."

He said, "I couldn't agree more."

She said, "Are you going to go out there?"

He said, "Yes, I was thinking of looking for the stones you saw."

She said, "Okay, be careful. People seem nice, but a little strange."

He said, "Strange? How?"

She said, "I don't think they get much interaction with the outside world. I just happened to be driving by there when I noticed their little festival. It's the only reason I stopped."

He said, "Interesting. Do you mind if we give you a call, in case we have any other questions?"

She said, "Not at all."

When we arrived back at the SUV, he said, "No offense to that lady. But people back then were into all sorts of weird crap. For all we know, she got her infection from smoking some bad peyote."

Both Joy and I laughed. We were fools.

Once John drove us out of the apartment parking lot, we headed to lunch. We didn't know it at the time, but restaurants close between lunch and dinner in Albuquerque. So it's good we left when we did.

We drove along until we spotted a nice sit-down Mexican restaurant. Well, a somewhat nice one. One that didn't have rats.

It actually took us a while. The part of Albuquerque we visited was flat with very little in it. But the journey was worth it. To be honest, the green chilies there were out of this world. Tasting one put you into another dimension.

Joy spotted an adobe building with a big bell on top and a taco in the window. It was perfect. When we walked up to its glass doors and walked inside, an older lady greeted us, wearing a Mexican party dress meant for someone much younger.

Walking across the cool Spanish tiles to a red leather booth, I admired the statues of donkeys and mariachis made from tin as well as the colorful ponchos draping the wall. The smell of fresh tortilla strips wafted up my nostrils.

After we sat down, ordered and finished eating, I excused myself to the boy's room. The inside was lovely. Tiles adorned the walls, sinks, mirrors and urinals, with several different styles and colors. One look and I knew I wanted the same brand of mezcal the designer drank.

When I left the bathroom, the sound hit me for the first time. As soon as I pushed the door open, the buzzing overwhelmed my senses. It prevented me from thinking clearly and interrupted my sense of balance. I sat down in front of the bathroom.

At first, I thought one of the insects from the old photographer's dead leg somehow survived and embedded itself in my ear. Relieved that even in my current state, this sounded absurd, I staggered to my feet and made my way back to the table.

John said, "You okay, sport?"

I guess I didn't look good. "Yeah, you know those chimichangas, they go right through you."

Truth was I felt like crap. I wanted to pay our bill and get back to the truck so I could rest. I fantasized about laying down in the back seat and sleeping for the next few hours.

Instead, I witnessed Joy and John's greatest argument of all time. Under normal circumstances, I didn't mind. When angry, Joy's beauty came to the fore. Her features sharpened. Her skin glowed with purpose. She was a hellion. A vengeful Valkyrie. Trick was getting her angry at someone else and not you.

The fight started when John mentioned going to the town featured in the photographer's pictures. Joy asked why he still wanted to go there.

She said, "Hey, we have the pictures we came for. Surely, we can just go back home. I'm sick of this place, anyhow."

John said, "What the hell are you talking about? We just got here."

She said, "So? We don't need anything else. We're just wasting money."

He said, "Well, if it's money, I told you, my dad…"

She said, "Screw your dad. I want to go home."

He said, "Well, that's not going to happen."

After going back and forth like this for what seemed like an hour, we paid our bill and left. The entire wait staff looked relieved when we walked out the door.

In the back seat of the truck, I laid down and looked up at the sky through the window. The New Mexico sky was so empty. And it went on forever. It made me feel hollow, like it sucked the soul out of me. What the hell was this place?

Maybe aliens did land here.

Truth be told, my anxiety was high. Between school and my fraternity, I found sleep difficult. Sometimes, I woke up in the morning with headaches. And my body ached, even after a long night's sleep.

Remembering the old photographer's insect-infested bones was another log on the fire of my unease.

Thinking of what the two geniuses argued about, I knew there was more to it than Joy let on. She was scared. We all felt it. Hell, I collapsed under its weight.

Looking back now, she was right. Leaving was the better option. Our only chance to save ourselves lay in leaving. And we ignored it. Poor Joy. The two men she needed most, let her down.

I dozed off to sleep. The New Mexico stars greeted me when I awoke in the evening. Seeing them shining in the black sky gave me a sense of peace. The New Mexico night was so different from the cold light of day. Turns out, New Mexico was enchanting after all.

With my eyes fixed on the stars, I saw them fade from view. Maybe a cloud crossed over the night sky, blocking them out. I don't know. But the entire sky turned black.

Still wondering what took the stars from me, I heard John announce, "Well, we have arrived!"

And that's when I knew we'd arrived in the little town of madness.

Chapter 6

MAD TOWN

There wasn't much in the mad town. Just a gas station, restaurant and motel.

Pulling into the parking lot of the motel, we saw five rooms facing the street and a neon welcome sign in the lobby window. All of us were tired. We yearned for sleep and didn't care where we put our heads.

When we walked into the lobby, we didn't see anyone, but there was a bell on the counter.

John rang it. "Anyone home?"

Turning to me, he said with a much quieter voice, "Maybe, we can just grab some keys and check ourselves in…"

We couldn't tell if he'd heard us or not, but a small, old man shuffled through a door behind the lobby counter. Did he ever stink! He smelled like raw eggs and mayonnaise left in the sun for days. As he lumbered towards us, I noticed his head and mouth twitching. He appeared as if he fought some sickness either in his mind or his body.

He said in a low voice, "Money."

John asked, "How much?"

And the old stinker pointed to the wall. There hung a list of prices for rooms on a board. John paid him for a single with two beds.

After handing us keys with hands so old the bones almost poked through them, he turned around and walked back to his office without as much as a *thank you.*

John said, "Service these days."

When we opened the door to our room, a stale smell greeted us. Turning on a lamp by the door, we saw a fine layer of dust on almost everything.

Lacking the energy to say more, John simply said, "Groovy."

After Joy and John announced they wanted the bed furthest from the window, I went to the bathroom. When I came back out and started to head to my bed, I looked over and saw the two of them getting it on. And, boy, were they ever getting it "on." Their whole bed shook and banged against the wall.

Since I didn't feel comfortable being this close to anyone's love making besides my own, I went back to the bathroom and perused my phone. Once or twice, I thought I heard voices coming from a small window above the toilet. But I wrote them off as motel employees leaving for the night.

After about an hour, I heard John say, "Hey man, you going to use the bathroom all night?"

I said, "Coming out."

I guess, Joy and John made up. I was happy for them. I didn't like the role of the third wheel when those two argued. I preferred the thought of an infestation of bugs in my bones over the awkward feeling that I needed to get along with them both while they yelled at each other.

The moment I laid down on top of the bed with my clothes on, I fell asleep. It was then that I experienced the funkiest dream of my life.

I stood standing on a mountain of ice, but further down below me, sand came bubbling out of the ground. Behind me I heard a scream. I turned around and saw Joy fall from my view. I heard her yell, "Don't forget me, dickhead!"

Turning back around, I saw arthropod forms carrying John's body in a bag with his face visible through a hole on its side. He was asleep. But I knew – just knew – they were taking him to some awful place. A place sane people didn't dare imagine.

Looking up in the sky, I saw a face. So horrible it was, my mind refused to remember it or give it form even now. I then heard a voice. A woman's voice.

It said, "Don't worry, child. You are at peace now. Don't be scared. We will remember you forever. In this way, you can rest. You served a purpose."

Suddenly, a loud buzzing took over the scene and drowned out everything I'd witnessed; the image before me, even the voice.

When I woke up, my head hurt, and my body ached. I felt even more tired than I had the night before. A migraine started to make itself known in my eye sockets.

Shielding my eyes from the sun streaming in from the window, I looked around the room for the source of the buzzing sound I heard. But I didn't see anything. I didn't recall John or Joy bringing an alarm clock either.

I whispered to myself, "Great way to start your day."

Our first goal of the day in the new town was getting something to eat. Opening our room door, we saw a cafe across the street. Without seeing its sign, we knew they called it the "Yellow Cafe," since someone covered every part of it in yellow paint, even its roof.

Sitting down at the first table we saw, we looked around for a server, but none came right away. Seeing the town for the first time in daylight, I noticed something peculiar about the town. Most people appeared young.

After a while, a young lady came to our table, but she just stood there looking at us. We stared back at her for a while until John broke the silence.

He said, "Three waters and some menus, please."

The girl stood there for a moment, smiled and then left. As I watched her run back inside and towards the kitchen, I saw some old crusty guy working in the kitchen. I thought, "Of course, the one place we see an unhygienic-looking old dude is in the kitchen of our restaurant."

After looking through the menus the young lady brought to us, along with our waters, we all decided on the green chili burger. We believed that of all the menu items, this one was the least damaging if something went wrong with the ingredients or cook time. The burger was quite good, actually. I tell you, those New Mexico chilis are out of this world.

When we received our check, John said to the young lady, "Are there any gift stores around here?"

She just looked at us and said nothing.

He said, "Here, look at this," and showed her one of the pictures from the photographer. "Do they still sell these images around here?"

But, without saying a word, she left.

Dumbfounded by her sudden departure, we looked at each other with raised eyebrows and glanced in the direction she'd walked in, only to see the ugly old man in the kitchen come out. I thought, "Oh God, not that guy."

Standing at our table, he looked terrible. His skin was old and gray and looked like it might fall off his bones. He said, in a voice eerily similar to the innkeepers, "Cassy Dumb. I help. Shop there." And he pointed to the gas station.

John said, "Over there is a gift shop?"

The old cook said, "Yes, flesh one."

I didn't know what was worse: talking to this geezer or shopping at a gas station. Nevertheless, after John laid down daddy's cash for the bill, leaving the restaurant and getting away from the smelly cook's kitchen made me happy.

The gas station was simple and aged. It came from a time long forgotten with its two pumps bleached by the sun to a pink color. In the desert heat, even walking the short distance from the Yellow Cafe to the gas station was a chore.

When we walked inside, a young man stood at the counter staring at us. He didn't say anything. He just looked at us with a blank face. I guess John's anger management classes paid off, since he didn't hit the dolt.

By now, we understood the town's culture – young people don't talk – so we looked for the souvenir section in the gas station by ourselves. When we didn't find anything, John rolled his eyes and said, "Here we go again."

To the dope, he pulled out the photograph and said, "Is this here?"

Predictably, the young man ran off, and we waited for the inevitable arrival of a smelly old person. Sadly, we didn't need to wait long.

Another skin-falling-off-the-bones oldie showed up and said in the same raspy, slow voice as the others, "Here, it is."

He took us to a section next to the counter which contained old postcards of the Smoky Mountains of all things. He cleaned off the dust from one of the lower shelves and handed a few wooden blocks with the image on it, just like in the photograph.

Looking them over in our hands, we didn't see any other markings or clues on the blocks. They answered nothing. We needed to ask the old guy some questions.

John said, "What is this picture? Where was it taken?"

The decaying gas station owner said, "Picture?"

John and I looked at each other with the same *What the hell?* expressions on our faces.

John said, "This picture! What is it?"

Again, the old guy said, "Picture?"

Traveling all the way from Cali to this hell hole in the sun to meet this dotard was beyond annoying. Thinking of the money and headaches made you want to punch this guy. I hoped John's anger management classes kicked in again.

His face turning red, John huffed and turned to the door. The classes had paid off yet again. Arriving back at the hotel, we all laid down on our beds and said nothing.

At that point, I figured our trip to hell town had ended. This was it. That time tomorrow, I saw myself on a plane headed back to SoCal.

Little did I know, however, mad town had so much more to offer. So much more.

Chapter 7

HELP WANTED

The next morning, we readied ourselves for the return home. I was relieved. Finally, we started our departure from this odd place of heavenly green chiles and hellish people. Unfortunately, the mad town decided a different destiny for us.

While Joy and I packed the bags, John went to the front office and closed out the bill. Whenever John was not around and I was alone with Joy, I avoided talking to her. I didn't like punches to the throat.

However, no sooner did John step out then he came back to the room. Excitedly, he said, "Change of plans! Joy, I think there's something we can do."

Both of us turned towards him with tired eyes. Being this close to leaving this awful, little town and then being told we decided to stay was bad news. Bad news indeed.

Joy said, "Okay, what is it?"

He said with a big smile, "The Yellow Cafe put up a help wanted sign."

Joy said, "Have you lost your mind? Those people are mutes! And the ones who can talk aren't human!"

He said, "C'mon, baby. We're this close. You can tell the locals are hiding something. That's why they've been so quiet. All you have to do is get close to them and we can find out where those stupid blocks came from."

She said, "No way."

He said, "Just apply. Give it a few days. If nothing comes of it, we can move on. I promise."

She said, "A couple of days?"

He said, "Yes, that's it!"

She said, "Okay, but at the first sign of something being screwed up, I am out of here and going back to Los Angeles, with or without you."

He said, "Fair enough."

Of course, no one cared what I thought. But I expected it. I was a freeloader after all. After they left, I opened the drapes and watched them walk to the cafe. This town was so oddball. When they entered the cafe, residents came out from the gas station and the motel and watched the restaurant. Like they all knew what was happening.

When Joy and John returned, all the residents scattered like bugs in the light. As he walked back to the hotel, I saw John smile. I frowned. No doubt, Joy scored the job.

Opening the door for them, even though I knew damn well the result I said, "What's the verdict?"

With Joy silent, John said loudly, "She got it! She starts tomorrow."

Poor Joy. My life sucked. But her life was worse. Tomorrow, her day started with a trip into the belly of the beast, with training sessions from gross people at a weird restaurant. And her pay was nowhere near enough to make up for it. Still, John hoped she might make new friends.

Chapter 8

CASSY

Joy's first friend in mad town was Cassy. Cassy was a runaway from Albuquerque. A forced relationship with a relative made her run away from home. Lucky for her, some friends took her in, and she found a job as a waitress. This hadn't lasted long thanks to a fight with her roommates, and she'd ended up on the streets. Life became harder as she drank and started using drugs. Finding a job became all but impossible due to her appearance. One look at her and people steered clear.

She wandered the streets of Albuquerque for some time until she decided to try her luck in Santa Fe. Hitching a ride from a trucker who pulled over his semi and started hitting on her less than halfway there, she jumped from the truck and ran up a road close to the highway. That's when she stumbled into the mad town. Her arrival was almost like fate.

If you're wondering how we found all this out, it's because Cassy told Joy. That's right. She wasn't a mute. Never was! Turns out, the society of mad town consisted of a weird hierarchical structure, where old people took in lost young people and gave them food and shelter. In return, the young people shut up and followed the instructions of the old.

The rotting grays even made promises of privilege to the young. If they followed the rules and let the old ones do all the talking when new people came to town, they also received peace of mind, eventually becoming grays themselves.

Joy said that her first day of work sucked. Big surprise. She said that no customers came in. Another huge shock. Eventually, with nothing to do, the cook made them clean the restaurant and then clean the kitchen after they'd closed. Most of the young people found this work challenging, but not Joy. In Los Angeles, she worked multiple jobs which required a strong stamina. Cleaning a restaurant for two hours after working all day was child's play for her.

While cleaning the crappers in the ladies' bathroom, Cassy started talking to Joy. She told Joy the story of her personal life. And she advised Joy never to talk to customers. Joy found her easy to tease, and asked, "Well what if my boyfriend is a customer?"

Cassy said, "No. Not even him."

Since Cassy seemed distressed that Joy had even asked this, Joy said, "Don't worry, I won't."

For the rest of the day, Joy joked around with Cassy. Joy loved teasing her and picking on her. She followed Cassy around, making things dirty again right after Cassy cleaned them. Having already journeyed the perilous journey of sobriety, Cassy was made of strong stuff, and she took this in her stride, playing along with Joy.

Joy asked her, "How long are you planning on staying here?"

Cassy shrugged and said, "I don't know. I like it here. It's peaceful. I don't worry about things like I used to. Maybe, if you stay here, you can also be happy."

When Joy came back to the motel last night, she was tired. But she was worried about staying in the mad town. She said to John, "Listen, we need to get the hell out of here. This place isn't normal."

John said, "What are you talking about? We aren't in hell. I know the people seem abnormal and the work is boring. But let's just give it a few days. You promised!"

She said, "This isn't about the work or the people. There's something wrong here."

John said, "How?"

30

She said, "There are only two types of people here: runaways and old bags of bones. Maybe, it's hell."

He said, "Well, it's great they are taking in runaways. I don't see that as a bad thing. And this place is old. No wonder there's old people around here. Stop being so worried about everything."

She said, "I am telling you. This place has dead-end written all over it."

And he said, "And I'm telling you we are going to leave in a few days. So don't worry."

At this, Joy went to the bathroom and took a shower.

I said, "John don't you think she has a point? I mean the old people around here look pretty crusty and gross."

He said, "Hey, man, they look like that all over America."

I said, 'Yeah, but they also talk weird and tell everyone else what to do."

He said, "Also, very much like the rest of America."

I said, "Are we really going to leave in a few days if we don't find anything?"

He said, "Of course, sport."

When they turned off the lights, Joy and John made up by banging the bed against the wall.

I doubted John's resolve in letting us leave in a few days. He was hellbent in finding the origins of the stupid carving. Money and notoriety drove him on. But, like Joy said, this place was a dead-end in more ways than one.

Although he expected Joy's job to produce investigative fruit, he wanted us to do some gardening ourselves. While she was at work, he wanted us to move around town and see what other information we could cultivate. We might just find a blossom of intrigue in this dead-end manure dump.

31

The next day, after Joy left for work, John and I went to the gas station for snacks and groceries. We were pathetic. Making our woman work while we ate candy bars was sad. When we walked in, we saw the same young man as before standing behind the counter. His name tag said, "Barry."

I said, "Morning, Barry."

As usual, Barry didn't say anything. But he looked worried. Uncharacteristic of the young people in town, his face didn't wear a smile and his brow was knitted into a frown.

I said, "You doing okay there, Barry?"

Without saying a word, he left the counter and went into the back. Shortly thereafter, a rotter came out and took up the counter.

I said to myself, "Well, that answers that question."

After going back to our room at the motel, John and I didn't talk much. I didn't fart very much either, since John looked in a real ball punching mood.

When Joy returned, she was not the same person. She acted strange. She kept quiet and wore a huge smile. Only after John asked her a question, did she start talking.

John said, "How did it go? Did you learn anything?"

She said, "Anything?"

John said, "Yes, the image. Did you find out about it?"

She said, "Yes."

John said, "Yes, what?"

She said, "Cassy and I talked about it at the Cabbage Patch."

John said, "You picked cabbage?"

"No."

He said, "Why did you go to a Cabbage Patch?"

She said, "To talk to people."

He said, "Oh my God, what people?"

She said, "The leaders."

At this, John paused. Joy was bizarre. She answered his questions like a robot with little or no explanation. And finding out Cassy had taken her somewhere strange without our knowledge made my hairs stand on end. I felt then like we'd bitten off more than we could chew.

John sat down next to her and held her hand. "Are you okay, honey? Anything we should talk about? Did Cassy's people do anything to you?"

Joy said, "I am okay."

That night, an eerie silence settled on our room. None of us joked around. And we all stayed in our own parts of the room without talking to each other. When the lights went out, the bed didn't bang on the wall.

The next morning before she left for work, John grabbed Joy and said, "Okay, you are not going to work. Take us to the Cabbage Patch you told us about."

Joy said, "But, I have work."

He said, "That restaurant is poisonous. I won't let you go."

She said, "You want to go to the Cabbage Patch?"

He said, "Yes, we have to find out what the hell is going on."

She said, "Work first and then I get Cassy and then Cabbage Patch."

John let go of her arm and thought about it. He said, "Okay, but you need to come back right away."

She said, "Okay."

After she left, John and I watched her walk to the restaurant from the window. Something wasn't right. I wanted to leave more than ever. Kidnapping Joy and leaving was a much better option than going to some cabbage patch.

We waited and waited. But Joy never returned. Panic grew in our motel room. And panic soon turned into anger. John said, "If they

33

have done anything to her, we are going to burn this moron town to the ground."

We walked to the restaurant. With his fists still clenched, John yelled, "Listen, you bastards, tell me where Joy is, or I am tearing this place to the ground."

A little old gray came out. He was different from the cook. He said, "I take you. Don't tear down, please."

As the rotter walked out of the restaurant, we followed close behind. Honestly, I didn't care where he took us. I just prepared myself to rock some heads. Unfortunately, my preparation failed to include my own head getting rocked.

Chapter 9

THE CABBAGE PATCH

The rotter looked like a member of the walking dead.

The gray guy took us to a place not far from town. It consisted of shacks and lean-to's- that looked a hundred years old. Dirt and mold covered the place, layering everything with a dark coat of grime inches thick. I felt like we stepped back in time to the old timey days.

John and I kept following Mister Zombie and prepared ourselves for anything. Our unspoken plan was the following: find Joy and kick ass, but not necessarily in that order.

Once we entered the grimy place, with shacks and lean-to's all around us, the gray guy said, "Wait here, I get."

John said, "What do you mean, 'wait here'? Where the hell are you going?"

He said, "I get her now. Bring to you!"

John paused. Both of us straightened our backs. The air turned thick with tension. Right below the surface of my anger, violence started to brew. Great bodily harm became a viable option. But we needed Joy.

John said, "Well, you better hurry and get her. Taking your time might be the last time."

The rotter ran off. John and I looked at each other. I whispered, "They could have guns."

John said, "Then we will take them from them."

After a few minutes, he said, "Let's move."

We stealthed around the place looking in the shacks. They were empty of life, with a few containing furniture.

We came across one with a person inside. A small figure was sitting in a chair with their head down.

John said, "Joy?"

The figure looked up. The person was a woman, but old and rotten like the others.

John said, "Ewww."

I said, "What the hell is this place?"

The thing in the chair said, "Cabbage patch."

I said, "Do you know where our friend is?"

It said, "Friend?"

I said, "Joy."

It began coughing. After the coughing continued for a while, I realized she wasn't coughing but laughing. A laugh with a throat and lungs long decayed by time.

It whispered almost to itself, "We take you. We take all of you."

I said, "Get your butt out of that chair. You are taking us to Joy."

It made a long coughing sound again and put its head back down.

John said, "Right, that's enough."

He took a step back and kicked the old lady right in the head. I gasped. Not because he kicked the old lady in the head. But because he kicked her head clean off. It went flying across the room and burst into a gray plume cloud of ash on the opposite wall.

John and I looked at each other and then back at the body. We saw a cloud of bugs fly out of the stump and out the door. Curious, we stepped closer and peered inside its neck. Just like the photographer's bones, its vertebrae contained holes. And inside these holes lay dead larvae and bugs.

John said, "No way."

I said, "This place is screwed."

We ran from the shack and yelled Joy's name. We stayed close to each other. No telling what kind of situation we were in.

I was frantic. Bugs, rotting old people and slimy buildings were out of my comfort zone. I felt sick and clammy, and my heart was thundering in my tightened chest. John also looked frazzled. But neither one of us said anything. We no longer pretended that we weren't scared

As we walked into one shack to look around, we heard a loud banging outside. After running out of the shanty and behind it, towards where the sound came from, we found a large shack. It was shaking. The noise came from inside.

We rushed to its door and flung it open. Both of us froze. It took us a moment to register what we were seeing.

Inside, at least a dozen people were engaged in an orgy. Young and old they piled on top of each other doing all sorts of unspeakable, bizarre acts. Mercifully, Joy was not among them.

John said, "What in the holy hell is that?"

He went to the door. And, before I yelled, "Don't!" he opened it.

At first, as the door swung free, nothing happened. Soon, however, all of the participants turned to the door and clamored towards John. Some of the old rotters ran on all fours. And some young ones, still with ecstasy in their eyes, staggered towards him like they were blind.

John slammed the door, and we ran for it. Behind us, we heard the door burst open and a chorus of moaning coming after us. Running between shacks to elude the mob, I yelled at John, "Don't ever open an orgy door again!"

Between breaths, he said, "I wasn't sure what it was."

We ran for almost an hour. Looking back, we saw nothing following us. Looking forward we saw the motel of the mad town up ahead. I said, "We get to our room. And then we get the hell outta here."

Although Joy was at the forefront of our minds, John and I were selfish. Self- preservation was key. Everyone sees themselves as a hero in situations like this. But when you're staring down death by orgy, your true nature will make itself known.

After Making it to our room, neither of us went for our bags. Instead, we grabbed our keys, wallets and phones and fled for the open door towards freedom. But standing there was someone we didn't expect.

Barry.

Chapter 10

BARRY

B arry spoke. He said, "Joy is in danger."

I said, "No shit."

He said, "No, they've taken her, just like they did my girlfriend. Joy asked too many questions. Now, she'll join "She Who Shall Not Be Named.""

I said, "Listen, once we get cell service, calling the authorities is the only thing that will save us."

He said, "By the time they get here, she won't even be bones. She will be dust."

Grabbing Barry by his collar and slamming him to the wall, John said, "Spit it out, bastard!"

Barry told us his story. He and his girlfriend were runaways. Someone they'd met at a party in Santa Fe told them about the mad town. And they traveled here for a guaranteed room and board.

Once here, he worked at the gas station; and she worked at the restaurant. In the beginning, they did as they were told. They kept their mouths shut and earned their keep by standing in empty buildings all day with no customers.

At a certain point, they knew the old ones wanted more from them. The mad townsfolk started talking to Barry and his girlfriend about growing old in the mad town and finding peace just like them. Neither of them wanted to stay that long, let alone long enough to grow old here. And that's when they said they wanted his girlfriend to meet "She Who Shall Not Be Named."

Barry never saw his girlfriend again. He looked for her all over. But the only trace he found of her was in a clearing near the Cabbage Patch. There, in a pile of white dust, he'd found her necklace.

He kept quiet and didn't make a show of his worry for her. The gray ones just kept telling him not to worry, they planned on giving him his moment of peace. Now, with us, he planned on escaping.

Taking time to understand our predicament, John and I experienced a change of heart. We discussed our plan with Barry and asked his advice. Our plan was simple: get some weapons and kick some ass. Barry told us there was a baseball bat in the hotel office and gasoline cans and lighters in the gas station. John told him to go to the gas station while we went to the hotel.

When we arrived at the front office, no one was there. The baseball bat was easy pickings. However, when we got to the gas station, Barry wasn't there. He'd bailed. Or the old rotters abducted him. In his stead, I grabbed a can of gasoline and some matches.

John and I walked slowly towards the cabbage patch. The sun went down and night crept in. Although we didn't have a flashlight, we knew the way.

And we knew what we must do.

As we walked closer to the Cabbage Patch, we witnessed a large group of hooded figures gathered in a clearing not far from the shacks.

John said, "Time to kick some ass."

As we made our way through the shacks on the way to the clearing, we noticed they were still empty. I started pouring gasoline on them. By doing this, we hoped to create a fire for our escape if we needed it.

Arriving at the outskirts of the clearing, we saw a bunch of hooded figures sitting on chairs in a circle. I said to John, "Oh my God, what a bunch of weirdos."

Walking out of the shadows, one of the hooded figures led a goat into the clearing. He started chanting. The seated figures started chanting as well. This went on for a good ten minutes until they all fell quiet.

Suddenly, we heard a great rumbling. John and I looked at each other and all around. At first, we didn't see anything and then the ground started bubbling up in the clearing. All sorts of rocks and roots and dirt came shooting out. After this, a few meters of sand bubbled out, and a horde of insects flew free from the dirt hole and into the night sky. Here and there, we saw the shadow of this swarm move through the sky, since it was darker than night.

Losing the swarm from sight, we heard a loud shrill and saw the goat bucking up and down. Bugs were all over it. They went into its eyes and nose and burrowed into its skin.

No sooner did the goat start screaming and kicking than an eerie silence took over the night. The goat stood there looking straight ahead. Looking closer, we saw it shaking a little, like it was trying to move itself.

John whispered, "Oh God."

I saw Joy walking towards the clearing. She didn't seem under duress. She actually appeared happy; smiling the whole time as she approached the ring of people.

Standing in front of the goat, she pointed her arms to the sky and chanted. Bringing her arms back down to her sides, she said something in the direction of the goat and a hooded figure stepped forward with a butcher's knife and hacked down on the back of the goat's neck.

In a terrific explosion of blood, the swarm emerged from the goat's neck like a firehose of gore and bugs. It went directly for Joy.

John screamed. But he was too late. The swarm engulfed her. He started running in her direction with his baseball bat.

I moved to go with him. But, as soon as I took one step, the buzzing hit me. I fell to my knees and then landed face first on the ground. No doubt caused by my anxiety, pain filled my head and nausea gripped my body. I managed to roll onto my side and look at John.

John swung his bat like a man possessed with the anger and tension of two thousand years of chaotic human history. He made contact with every single head around him. And when he did so, most of the heads exploded into dust. You knew he hit someone young when the bat made a dull thump instead of popping.

He shouted things like, "Die, Bastards!" and "Suck on this!"

I saw John take out at least ten of the bastards. Even after he felled his prey and scattered their friends, he kept swinging and shouting into the air. Once he exhausted himself, he fell to his knees, panting. About this same time, I recuperated and clamored to my feet. Making my way to where John was, I looked around. I couldn't see Joy anywhere.

I said to John, "Where's Joy?"

Without looking up, he pointed to an area in front of us. I walked to it. Looking down, I didn't want to understand what I saw. There among the blood, the bodies and the bugs, was a skeletal cage with a human face still attached. Actually, it was a whole human head. It was Joy's. Nausea rose up inside of me and the world spun fast.

Thinking she was dead; I jumped back and fell down when she smiled at me and winked. In a raspy voice, she said, "It is so peaceful. You must join us. You too can live forever."

While I sat and stared at her beautiful face and eyes which stared back at mine, John walked up beside her and brought the bat down on her head. It made a squishing sound as it expelled fluids out of the eyes and what was left of her chest. He said, "That bitch is not my Joy."

He helped me up. As we walked back to the shacks, we set them on fire. We didn't worry so much about covering our escape. Rather,

42

we just wanted to destroy the evil swarm from hell. We watched as the flames jumped from shack to shack and then we started our walk back to town. Just as we cleared the last of the shacks, we heard a weak voice say, "In here. In here."

Startled that one of the things lived and wanted our help, we went looking for it. Inside one of the shacks not yet on fire, we looked in and saw Barry. He sat up against one of the shack walls. Next to him was Cassy. Cassy was too far gone. Looking at her idiot smile and bright eyes, we knew we were too late to save her. Barry said, "Smoky Mountains."

John said, "What?"

Barry struggled to speak. Doubtless, the things' invasion of his body and mind was close to complete. In a weak voice he managed to say again, "Smoky Mountains."

Most likely insane from losing his girlfriend, John said, "Smoke on this." And he brought the bat right down on Barry's head, crushing it. Looking at the carnage John just unleashed, we saw bugs make their way out of the gore of the top of Barry's head and spring into flight.

John yelled, "Goddamn Bastards!"

After running outside, we saw the bugs fly into a larger group of bugs which flew away into the night sky. The hideous darkness of the swarm cast a mocking shadow on the cool, clear New Mexico night.

I said, "That's what he was trying to tell us. They are going to the Smoky Mountains. Wherever the hell that place is."

Neither of us said a word until we arrived back at our motel room and John said, "Next stop, the goddamn Smoky Mountains."

Chapter 11

THE GREAT SMOKY MOUNTAINS

John had lost his mind. He kept talking about the image like nothing had happened. Any fool knew his behavior was abnormal. So, I tried to force the issue with him. I asked him whether we should tell Joy's parents or not. I asked him about her work and if we should let them know. But he said nothing.

I watched the news. There was no mention of a fire – or a mass slaughter – in the small town which I called mad town. People only care about things they know. And, with the exception of a few college students on a scavenger hunt or a couple of runaways who the world no longer cared for, most people had never heard of the mad town.

I foresaw a census taker or a road crew fixing a highway in the area stumbling across the mad town one day. Until then, however, their fate was our secret.

Truth be told, I missed Joy. We were not fast friends. But, I think because of this, her death hit me twice as hard. Before all of this, I daydreamed about her being gone. I fantasized about getting back the days when John and I spent time together without her.

Now, with her no longer around, I looked for her everywhere. When we took the SUV to the airport, I jumped in the backseat, still thinking she would sit in front. When we boarded the plane, I left the seat empty for her next to John. And in my actual dreams, I saw her clear as day, staring back at me.

Finding the Great Smoky Mountains was easy. It is one of the largest mountain ranges in America. But this also presented us with a problem. If I wanted to wipe the bugs from the face of planet earth, how would we find them? And, even if we did, how could we wipe them out in such a vast area?

I said to John, "We need to give up on this. It's over. We need to go back to LA and work on our alibis. People are going to be asking about Joy."

He said, "You know what you are without me? A nothing. One big nothing. We are going to find something and then we can stop. If you want to leave, fine. If you want to stay, then shut up."

No one likes someone calling them nothing. But I chalked this up to John having lost his mind. I needed to stick with him. That's what friends do, right? Besides, John and I were thick as thieves when it came to slaughtering towns and causing the sacrifice of one's girlfriend.

When we landed in Asheville, the damp ground and dark skies foretold our doom. How could a swarm migrate this far from a desert? Obviously, they held some kind of supernatural power. A power greater than any we'd gained in our undergraduate studies.

The story of North Carolina was a simple one. Not necessarily inhabited by the simple, but owning a simple history, nonetheless. One of the oldest states in the union with a rich farming history. All of its prosperity was lost to foreign growers.

Adapting to the change, the people there became truckers. In some rural areas, they also pursued jobs as handymen. And, where this failed, they sometimes turned to welfare and drugs.

As we made our way to the car rental terminal, I begged John not to get an SUV again. Of course, I didn't tell him why. I didn't want anything that reminded me of Joy. Predictably, he ignored me and rented another one. He was clearly in complete denial of our situation and what happened to us.

We drove and drove along a highway empty of other cars and lined by green trees in all directions. The moisture in the air smelled sweet.

It made me ponder what the earth was like when it was young. And just how long those goddamn bugs had existed on it.

Arriving in Hendersonville, we took up residence at a bed and breakfast. John paid for the top floor for the whole week. In retrospect, this was a huge waste of cash, but at least it gave me something to come back to.

We went to dinner at a local cafe. Actually, the food was good. Evidently, the chef started a restaurant there catering to tourists escaping the Florida heat.

John told me his new plan. He'd researched the Smoky Mountains on the internet. And he found a professor who studied the archaeology of the mountains. He intended to visit her dig sites and see what they offered.

We didn't need to get too close to her sites, since he'd bought a drone from a local store for flying over the area as well as camping gear for observing anything we found for days from a distance. Using his dad's credit card, I also purchased a ton of pesticides and guns, just in case.

That night, as we slept in the bed and breakfast, I marveled at how close the ceiling rafters hung above my bed. It reminded me of my fraternity cage. To distract myself, I remembered a story about a spell-wielding rat living in the attic space and terrorizing the residents as they slept. This was folly, however. Nothing was more horrific than my current circumstances. Not even a horror writer dreams of something that bad.

The next morning, we woke up and split. Even though our camping gear included rations, we bought some snacks to tide us over until we set up our camp.

As John floored it down the freeway, like he was pursuing a death wish, I put my feet on the dash and looked out the window. Storm clouds brewed overhead. Our first camp night promised rain.

As I looked towards the horizon, I saw it. I know I did.

A beast. A black insect which spanned the skies.

It threatened the land, maybe even the world. Madness stormed through my mind. Were the bugs eating my brain?

Remembering that Joy used to put her feet on the dash, I put my feet back on the floor. Looking again out the window, I saw only black clouds.

I stared at the road in front of me. I envisioned John and I riding into the tunnel of a storm. In his insanity, John was right. Our only path forward was our end. All roads lead to this. Going home was a detour on the road to our demise. For the first time in my life, I prayed to God.

I said, "Lord, give me strength. Help me and I will give you the most epic pest extermination of all time."

John looked at me with hard eyes and didn't speak. He thought I was joking. I wasn't. I didn't know how to pray. I was godless.

John worried me. Even before all of this, reading him was hard. Now, I found understanding him impossible. No telling what was in his mind. Running out of time scared me. Destroying the swarm required John's sanity. His falling off the deep end spelled trouble for us all.

We turned off the highway onto a gravel road. Following this for a few miles lead to a parking lot. After getting out our camping gear, guns and pesticide, we started walking down a trail next to the lot. A ranger by some bathrooms yelled some advice to us. We ignored him. I felt like telling him, "I have some advice for you. Don't follow us. And, if you never see us again, count yourself blessed."

It started sprinkling with rain. I said, "Well, that's great."

John didn't say anything. Normally, Joy told me to screw myself in such circumstances. Her absence hung in the air. I felt its mass and it drained me. Looking at John, it seemed to have hit him as well. His head hunched over. He looked down at his feet and kept walking.

We hit the trees and walked on. Knowing strong rains looked down from above, we set up camp in a clearing. When the rain drops thudded on the roof of the tent, I hoped John found rest that night. With his mind gone, he was like a child. He didn't understand our predicament. Our remaining days and nights on earth were few indeed.

Chapter 12

DR. JOYCE

D r. Joyce was my crush. She was everything I was not. Strong, worldly, smart, you name it. A glance at her profile picture made me feel warm and safe.

Somehow, my phone received a signal in this part of the Smoky Mountains. With rain thundering on my tent and a menace to the entire human race outside of it, I decided to surf the web and understand why John followed Dr. Joyce.

Her website explained everything. Like us, she went to a world-renowned university. Unlike us, she'd graduated. Upon her graduation, she traveled to South America and studied ancient races. Her expertise was in other-worldly hieroglyphics of extinct civilizations. By other-worldly, I mean images of flying saucers.

For some unknown reason, she packed up and moved to the Smoky Mountains. She continued to study lost cultures, keeping her work a secret. Intriguing indeed!

Everyone needs saving. I was overdue. I was in a very vulnerable position. One friend sacrificed and the other, crazy. I was manic about my own sanity.

Dr. Joyce was worth our trust. She checked all the boxes. Like us, she was educated. She investigated mysterious beings. She was in the Smoky Mountains.

Besides, she was hot. Voluptuous black hair, sharp cheekbones, piercing hazel eyes. She checked all my boxes.

In my fantasy encounter of our first meeting, we sat down together. We talked about all my current problems. In a super calm, delicate manner, she offered advice in a soothing voice. She hugged me as I cry. She saved me from the world-destroying insect swarm.

Hey, when you are staring down the end of the world, you look for someone stronger. Judging from her picture, Dr. Joyce was stronger than Joy. She was like a super-Joy.

On her website, she'd marked several sites of interest. The Smoky Mountains were huge. Even if an army told you their exact location, you might miss them. The trees were dense too. The sound of a shotgun blast travelled less than one hundred yards.

Since John didn't t tell me where he wanted to go first, I made an educated guess. The nearest site on Dr. Joyce's website was a prospect of hers. She planned on visiting it again. This site was untouched for the most part.

This was a good site for John and me. Marked by a certified archaeologist and vacant, the location seemed promising. I didn't worry about seeing Dr. Joyce. Meeting her was my dream but a dream worth the wait. Not everyone wants their dream to come true right away. That's what makes it a dream. Reality can ruin it for you.

Chapter 13

THE MUD CAVES

Dr. Joyce left the Mud Caves behind because accessing them was difficult. She wrote of the age of the strata at the bottom of the caves. They were millions of years old and rivaled any ancient rock formations in the Americas. Getting to the bottom of them was another story.

John sent up his drone. Far above the Smoky Mountains, the whole area for miles looked like one large piece of broccoli. Finding anything in this place deserved a medal. As we moved the drone closer to the cave site, cliffs and a waterfall revealed themselves to us.

Above the cliffs, a series of buildings appeared in the distance. Due to their distance from the waterfall, they were not a concern but would be worth looking into later.

At the bottom of the waterfall, dead trees lined its stream. John landed the drone in the clearing left by the fallen trees. Rocks blocked the camera's view. Hovering and then landing the drone to turn it without changing its position, John mapped a three-hundred-and-sixty-degree view of the clearing.

After John moved the drone back ninety degrees and flew it close to the cliff wall, he landed the drone again in front of a cave. The cave was narrow and a few feet off the ground. Making a decision was necessary, Fly the drone into the cave and risk losing it or pack up camp and hike to the cave.

John said, "I don't want to go back to town for another drone. And that opening looks like the butt crack to hell."

Flying the drone along the ground back to the clearing, John steered it upward avoiding the trees, and he flew it back to our camp. After recharging, he targeted the buildings from earlier.

After flying straight for ten minutes, the drone descended to the buildings. Located next to the river which ran over the cliff, the area appeared devoid of life. No people, no activity, nothing.

The drone landed. As John steered the drone around in a three-hundred-and-sixty-degree radius like before, all the buildings appeared locked. Their doors and windows were shut.

The drone moved closer to a building in front of it. The building was old. The eaves drooped over the door. Its stairs were broken. The place seemed abandoned.

John hit the return key on the drone. "Well, that's it. Let's pack it up and go to the caves."

Rain drops started falling again. I didn't say anything this time.

While we walked through the forest, fog rolled in. With rain, trees, rocks and an uneven slope, this was not a great place for walking in fog. I said, "Maybe we should stop for a bit. I don't want to break my butthole falling on a rock."

John said, "Screw that. This fog's not breaking. Let's keep going and see if we can walk out of it."

Even with the use of a compass, marching on became harder and harder. The fog swirled around us and blocked out the sky. Losing an eyeball on a tree limb or breaking an arm from a fall were not out of the question. Losing sight of John, I called out, "Hey, man, are you there?"

He yelled, "Woah, shit!"

Hearing a rustling sound followed by falling rocks, I stopped walking and looked in the direction of the noise. Seeing through the fog was impossible.

I yelled, "Hey, man, you okay?"

No answer.

Slow, sure steps took me to where John last stood. Less than a foot in front of me was a steep drop down a hill. Leaning over, I yelled, "John, you down there?"

I heard him yell back, "Yeah. I made it out of the fog. If you go to your right a little, it's a little less steep."

After making my way over like he said and going down the slope, I said, "This is too easy."

There was no fog at the bottom. Seeing far was possible. John stood less than fifty yards from me.

He walked to me and said, "One hell of a ride. Express way to hell. But, worth it." He pointed in front of him. Not far from where we stood, the waterfall was visible.

I said, "You can thank your sweet ass for that. Let's find a camping spot before the rain starts coming down hard or the fog decides to follow us."

As we walked towards the clearing, the earth gave way to more rocks and gnarled fallen trees. Even though a river ran through it, the clearing was empty of vegetation.

A spot on the edge of the clearing with some trees provided shelter and a place to put our tents. The rain prevented us from making a fire. The coming night promised cold food and cold bodies.

Checking my phone reception confirmed there was no signal. Even though it provided me with emotional support in the form of Dr. Joyce's web page, surfing the web was not a good option. Better to conserve our batteries in case of emergency, even with our backup power. No telling how many days inspecting the caves required.

Long before nightfall, we each separated into our respective tents. These days, neither one of us talked much. Nothing made sense.

Justifying our search was futile. Calling the police and notifying Joy's parents was the rational, responsible choice. Unfortunately, good or bad, following John's decisions was my life's credo.

While staring up at the roof of my tent, I heard a low chorus of voices cut through the rain and trees. The chant was identical to what we heard in the mad town. Not dissimilar in tone and number, the chorus was disconcerting. It sounded ominous.

Sitting up in the tent and raising my voice loud enough for him to hear me, I said, "Hey, John, you hear that?"

He answered, "Yeah."

"How far, you think?"

He said, "Far."

I said, "You think it's those buildings we saw?"

"No way, those were empty. It's far off, probably farther than the buildings or in a different direction."

I said, "What if they came from under the ground?"

He said, "That's the bugs and not the people, dummy."

I said, "Yeah."

I didn't ask him the less pressing question of why we were even there. Getting him to talk or make conversation about our immediate problems was hard enough.

The chorus continued for an hour and came to a sudden stop. Relieved at its silence but concerned what might come next, we panicked when the ground shook.

The earthquake was not subtle. It was strong, violent and sustained. It capsized our tents with us inside. It prevented us from standing up or moving besides rolling on the ground.

We both screamed and yelled. In fear of my life, I fought the urge to tell John what an idiot he was in bringing us here.

When the earthquake stopped, both of us lay wrapped in our tents. We moaned, with hurt butts and heads. After unwrapping ourselves and finding some flashlights, we sorted out our gear.

I said, "Stay here?"

He said, "Of course, genius. Earthquakes travel for miles, and we can't walk in the dark."

Again, I resisted the urge to call him an idiot. I wasn't worried about dying from the earthquake. Our foe was not just physical, they were supernatural. Who knew their potential?

I put my tent back up. Almost everything was wet. At least we'd followed good camping techniques and put our electronics in Ziploc bags.

Dreading the morning and wondering what bad crap it had in store for us, I was restless. Sleeping was impossible. As I look back now, that night was the saddest of my life. It was the last night I spent with John.

Chapter 14

DEEP DOWN, A GREAT DISASTER

At the bottom of those goddamn caves, disaster waited for us. Nothing else. John's days ended without him finding any answers. Our day started the same as all the days around that time. We rose, packed our stuff, and ate a little. All without saying a word. When he wanted us to take our next step, John spoke.

He said, "Another day, another dollar. This is it, sport. The big one! I can feel it!"

Thinking back on it, I sigh at the irony of his last words before we set out on our final adventure together. Too bad for him, his dollar earning days were over. He was right about it being the big one.

Walking up to the cave's mouth, we jumped up to enter it. Neither one of us knew the art of spelunking. John's gear included climbing equipment which required training to use. Like most people, our cave training was from shows on television.

At the cave's mouth was a large cavern. Standing up or storing our gear in it was not a problem. What looked like dry mud covered the walls and floor. Preserved rock patterns resembling dried rain puddles gave the caves a muddy appearance and their name. There were two exits. One large and one small.

Once we lightened our load, we headed for the large exit. This one led to an easy and short exploration. As we walked through it, it opened up into another large cavern with one exit. Exploring this one a little and then heading through the exit, we entered a tunnel big enough for two people to comfortably walk down.

This was awesome! Who said spelunking was hard?

At the end of the corridor was a small room and nothing else. A dead end. When we looked around in it, signs of someone having been there were evident. Leaving footprints on the floor and markings on the walls, they'd searched for something.

I sniffed the air, hoping for a brief whiff of Dr. Joyce's perfume. The putrid smell of mold and mildew greeted me. *Better luck next time*

We turned around and headed back towards the cave's entrance. The realization of our next destination hit me. The small exit from the first cavern. Entering that hole required turning sideways and ducking. No telling what lay beyond it.

I said, "Uh, John, whoever was here before stayed in the cave we just left. Maybe, there's nothing in that small hole we saw earlier."

He didn't say anything. Typical John response. For him to get what he wanted, ignoring me was the easiest option.

Arriving at the opening, he said, "I will go first."

He was brave. The hole was small and dark in a mountain, miles from civilization. Going first took balls of steel.

The tunnel was tight. Tighter than an ass with one cheek. As we ducked our head lights below a low ceiling and squirmed to get around tight corners, calling our journey difficult was an understatement. My sweat proved instrumental in helping me squeeze through. For our reward, we found a hole in the cave floor about the size of a man.

I said, "Screw that, John. That has dark, suffocating death written all over it."

He smiled and said, "It's the price of admission."

Oh brother. When he pounded some hooks into the opening and attached rope, we both knew his intention. My anxiety came on strong. Following him down the hole seemed impossible.

Once he'd disappeared from sight, reviewing my options became easier. Following him wasn't mandatory. Returning to camp sounded really good.

Standing there with inaction as the best option, I heard her. Joy. I was crazy. No doubt about it. But I still heard her.

She said, "Go."

What a jerk. Even in death, she told me what to do. What did I owe her? Actually, quite a lot. Even if she gave me a death wish.

As I climbed down the hole, thinking about Joy helped. Looking down was hard. The head light bumped against the sides of the hole. I took a leap of faith. Getting stuck or falling to my doom were distinct possibilities. Believing in Joy was my inspiration to go on.

As I crawled down the hole, it became narrower. Stretching my arms above me and my legs below, I wriggled down the tight hole. Turning more to my left than John had was a disastrous mistake. Halfway down the hole, in the darkness with my outstretched body bumping into rocks, I became stuck. The rocks prevented me from moving my body around.

Stuck in the dark, hundreds of feet below the earth's surface. My predicament promised a long, lonely and painful death. Remembering my days in the fraternity cage, I panicked. I started kicking and banging my arms and head. Blood trickled down my face. I heard a loud buzzing sound and passed out.

As I came to, everything around me was still black. Below me, John said, "Are you there? Talk to me!'"

"I'm here."

He said, "Can you make it down? Neither one of us can get out of here until you get out of the hole."

I said, "I don't know."

"Try turning!"

I said, "I did."

Neither of us said anything then. My final act on planet earth was killing both of us. As I accepted my fate, my body relaxed. My limbs loosened and permitted my body to turn. When I rotated to the left, my body slid the rest of the way down the hole.

After climbing out of the ceiling of the cave, I landed on its floor. Our rope dangled from the hole above us. Illuminated by my headlight, sand covered the entire floor.

John said, "Good of you to join us."

I said, "Why's it covered in sand?"

"I don't know. Let's look for another opening."

I said, "I can't go on anymore. I don't know if I can make it back up."

He said, "If you want to leave, then leave."

I sat down. This room was small and weird. It was a dead end as far as I was concerned. There was no point in going on. John was a dick.

John said, "Hey I found another hole. I'm going in."

When I looked in the direction of his voice, the last thing I saw was John's feet wriggling into a hole in the wall. Following him was dumb. I contemplated our situation. Waiting for John was the most responsible thing to do. Getting the hell out of here was the smartest thing to do.

The ground shook me from my contemplation. The whole room started heaving. Rocks dropped from the ceiling. Another earthquake started.

I ran over to the hole and yelled into it, "John it's time to go! This place is coming down!"

I heard a faint voice say, "Screw you. I am going on."

The earthquake grew more intense. Rocks slid down the hole. Standing up was difficult. The room collapsing on us was not out of the question. I panicked and jumped onto the rope above me, pulling myself up. Due to my fear of dying, my arms found new strength. I sucked air in and tried to make myself thinner. My will to survive pushed me to safety. My recollection of how to turn my body helped in negotiating the hole a second time.

Making it to the top, I yelled down, "John, come on!"

I heard nothing except rocks falling.

Wiggling down the narrow tunnel to the main cavern proved difficult. The walls on either side threatened to crush me. My feet didn't move fast enough.

Once I made it to the mud caves, I sprinted for freedom. After running straight for the cave opening, I threw my body out of it, into the cold dusk of late afternoon. Landing on the ground with a, "Whommpf," I jumped to my feet and aimed for the tree line.

Throwing myself backwards onto our camping supplies, I heard a loud rumbling. The earthquake intensified. It became fatal. Trees fell down. Water came out of the river. Entire boulders rolled off the cliff. I grabbed my gear and hung on for dear life.

A huge explosion ripped through the mud caves, blowing out meters of rocks and sand. Only divine intervention spared me from a large boulder landing on top of me. The sand blanketed the river in front of it, damming it and causing the waterfall to fill the ground around the clearing.

Believing the worst was over, I was caught off guard by a second explosion. Its quick, sharp veracity startled me and made me pray for my dear soul. Instead of boulders or sand coming out of the cave this time, an enormous swarm of bugs emerged. They blackened the darkening sky and bounded for the cliffs.

Beneath the falling rocks and trees, I heard a faint chorus of chanting coming from over the waterfall.

Bastards.

When the earthquake and chanting stopped, my thoughts turned to John. Thinking he'd survived was ridiculous. Searching at night for his remains would not be practical. I waited for daylight.

As I surveyed the area in the morning, the perfect word to describe the wreckage was Armageddon. Boulders lay on top of trees, crushed into sticks by the weight. Sand and trees dammed the river and separated it into three streams.

After walking around with my head swiveling left and right, my neck hurt. Sitting down on a fallen tree, I put my chin in my hands. Deep in thought, I didn't see what was right in front of me. As my thoughts cleared, my eyes focused. John's shoe stuck out of some rubble not five yards from me.

Walking over and pulling his shoe, I screamed when his whole leg came out.

I threw his leg away from me. Refusing to take my eyes off of it for fear it might start walking, I sat down hard in the dirt.

That poor bastard. Now I was two friends down.

I was alone.

Being able to call my own shots was not a boon for me. I was confused and scared.

What the hell was it with the chanting? Did that summon the bugs? Did it control them? Did it summon something else?

Under a group of fallen trees lay John's backpack. Pulling the insides out, my hand touched his wallet. A bulging leather monstrosity, his wallet was fat. Flicking through the greenbacks, I counted a couple of thousand dollars in addition to the credit cards. John was the posthumous financier of my solo adventure.

Even though this was stealing, something told me John was fine with me taking the money. John told me to come here. Joy died because of John. All of my present problems were his fault. Continuing on towards my own demise was something he wanted.

I Powered up my phone and it advised me of my next destination. On the home screen, my open browser showed Dr. Joyce's profile. She was my savior. Finding her was my chance for survival and redemption for Joy and John.

Chapter 15

DESTINATION SALVATION

The sun fell on my tent in the morning. Without the shade of the trees, my tent received the full blast of the sun's rays. The heat of these rays forced me awake, turning my little tent into a ready-made bake oven.

After spending most of the prior day in dark rumination after finding John's remains, I took a quick tour of the ruins upon awakening. For the first time, I noticed several red boulders. Walking over to them, I determined a large amount of red liquid covered them, giving the boulders their color.

Underneath those boulders, John's remains lay. Or at least the small amount of John which hadn't been squashed. Moving one step closer to those boulders was out of the question. Turning my body in a complete one-hundred-and-eighty-degree angle and moving back in the direction I came from, I put out of my mind the grisly scene. Out of sight, out of mind, they say.

Something that smelled like a wet animal wafted through the air. With his inert body, John's last act on the planet was an odor. I wondered if this was the last act of all of us when the time came. Praying to God for a rose-scented odor when I die, I distracted myself from the fate which awaited me.

Trying to avoid looking behind me as I packed up the remnants of our gear, my eyes chanced upon a shine coming from the base of one of the fallen trees. Walking to it, my feet kicked a stone with an image on it.

Well, screw me sideways! There it was. The object of John's quest in all its glory. Staring back at me from the ground, the hideous, menacing image first seen in Japan. Up to now, we viewed only pale, internet copies of the original. I have to say, upon seeing an original, I understood John's determination in finding it.

It was old. Beyond old. If this existed prior to humanity, it was invaluable. Priceless. Its presence put all of history in doubt. All of evolution. Finding it in two places so far from each other spoke of something more than chance.

Putting it in my pack, I said out loud, like John was listening, "Don't worry, sport, I know where to take this. This is for you and Joy."

After checking Dr. Joyce's website on my phone and true north on my compass, I headed out in the direction of her last known location.

While I walked, I screamed and yelled. Victory was mine. With nothing around to hear them, my cries of relief and joy bounced off the trees unnoticed. They were as free as me.

Barring an encounter with a bear or becoming lost, my estimated arrival at Dr. Joyce's camp was two days. The Smoky Mountains are a scary place. All sorts of bad things happen to people there. Stories abound of cannibalistic wild men, child-kidnapping sasquatches, and homicidal pot growers.

With a .45 in my hand and DDT in my pack, I smiled. For man, beast or insect, my aim was true. Only those seeking a quick, complete annihilation begged to cross my path.

My ammo was high grade. Putting dum dum bullets in my sidearm and filling balloons with DDT powder, my goal of hell on earth took a step closer to reality. In a way, I itched for a fight. Much like a cornered animal, the world left me no choice.

Making camp on a small overhang above a shallow cave gave me a strategic advantage in case of visitors. Lighting a fire with a stone border also ensured no smaller callers rummaged through my supplies.

When I went to sleep that first night, my pistol lay across my chest; and my balloons nested themselves in a stack by my pillow.

When I heard the first sound, I credited it to squirrels looking for morsels. Thinking of little animals like these scavenging on John's remains, I forced myself back to sleep.

The second time I heard something, I said, "Okay, A-holes. Let's party."

As I breached the front of my tent, I heard distinct footsteps behind me. At a quick guess, I estimated two or three people. Crouching low and turning, I fired two shots. My first was blind. My second was also blind but three feet to my right.

I guessed right. Both shots struck gold. The first blowing some a-hole off his feet. The second hit a robed figure who burst into dust.

Seeing the bugs form in cloud above the stack of vacated clothes, I threw one of my DDT bombs at the ground below them. When the balloon exploded into a cloud of DDT, the insects spun around confused, and flew off into a southerly direction.

I said, "Take that to your masters, crickets."

Without cleaning up my mess, I went back into my tent and lay back down. The forest always cleans up dead messes.

In the morning, I kicked out the burning embers of my fire and packed up my gear. Looking over at where their remains lay, I wondered about the two jerk-offs.

Were they like me and John? Did they know what happened to them? Did they even know they died?

I set off again for true north and the meeting of my dream. Confident last night, I was even more confident now. Getting a few bug-kills under your belt does that.

So far, the crickets only came out at night. What was up with that? Did they hate sunlight? Was it some sick, macabre cult crap?

After gaining a hill, an unabated view of the Smokey's appeared over my shoulder. With the sun reflecting off the branches of thousands of trees into the distance, The Smokies were beautiful. Its history was ancient.

If you believe some of the histories made up by television shows, knights and romans came to the mountains thousands of years ago. Imagine the expressions on their faces when bugs flew up their asses after arriving in the new world. That would be something worth traveling back in time to see. It was also a better idea for a television show.

Camping at night was not an option. Marching through the night was a must. The bugs were still out there, waiting for nightfall and a chance to even their score with me.

Tonight, increasing their numbers to an army of creatures was their best chance of success. I doubled my pace. Making quick time through the day was necessary to stay ahead of them. The night was an advantage for mindless abominations who didn't feel pain regardless of terrain.

It was hard work climbing through mountains. The temptation to keep taking breaks was strong. I felt exhausted within hours of hiking. I pushed myself on. Marching day and night were my only chance for survival.

Imagining a horde of insects hot on my butt, I lamented the problems I was bringing to Dr. Joyce. I wanted our first meeting to be perfect and not a perfect disaster.

As nightfall approached, my fear grew. I knew those bastards wanted me in the worst way. I panicked. I started running as fast as possible. Almost breaking my ankle a few times, I strove on.

At dusk, I climbed a small hill nearby, trying to get above the trees' canopy. Far off in the distance from the direction of my last camp, I saw the trees shaking.

The bugs were pissed.

The large buzzing sound overtook me. I crumpled next to a tree.

Knowing the bugs' plans for me forced me back to my feet. Grabbing a branch of the tree and pulling myself up, I said, "Screw this," and started my trek through the night forest.

After turning on my headlight, checking my compass and making a mental note of the stars, I hauled ass down a hill. Thankfully, at the bottom was an old set of train tracks leading in the direction of Dr. Joyce. Gods be praised!

With my gun at my side, and balloons in my pockets, my defenses were short range at best. Their use required the small insect army to overtake me. In such a scenario, I didn't stand a chance against overwhelming numbers.

Despite their age, the timbers of the train tracks proved sturdy enough for my continued escape. Heaven sent indeed! If I survived the night, I counted finding these tracks as my best luck ever.

Jog-walking over ruts, even traversing the tracks was hard work at night. Hoping they lead all the way to the good doctor was lunacy. At some point, leaving them was necessary. Going up a hill with a million crickets up my arse was not a pretty picture.

After a good six hours on the tracks and no sound of pursuit, dawn was only hours away. My chances of escape were good.

The tracks ended. My chances of escape became worse. Looking underneath the tracks,. I saw a riverbed about fifteen feet below them. The river was flowing in the doctor's direction as well.

Hanging from the tracks and then dropping the rest of the way, I landed on the riverbed and ran for it. Slipping here and there on rocks, my feet still managed a good escape. I was blessed twice that night.

At the end of the riverbed stood a steep hill. Climbing by taking large steps and pulling on trees, I heard something off in the distance.

The sound was like a roar. As I listening hard, it came again. It wasn't a roar. It was an amalgamation of hundreds of angry insects.

Despite fatigue, sore ankles and a lack of nutrition and rest, I pushed myself hard up the slope. Praying to God the whole time; I made all sorts of promises impossible for me to keep.

Making the top of the hill, I saw it! Dr. Joyce's tent was a couple of hundred yards in front me. I'd made it! Or so I thought. Looking behind me, my eyes set on a huge, black mass moving over the riverbed, blocking the terrain from view. Looking closer, I saw all sorts of insects and humanoid creatures. Crickets, humans, bugs with legs, humans with insect legs. Holy crap, those bastards came in all sorts of sizes and shapes. Madness!

I bounded down the other side of the hill, yelling, "Doctor. Save me! Save me."

When I arrived at the bottom of the hill, my legs gave out. Falling forward into a roll, I sprang back up into a run, without wasting any time. To my left, the sun peeked over the trees. The heat of its rays filled the forest.

I yelled, "Not today, assholes!"

Trees blocked my view of the doctor's camp. I ran on faith. While giving myself fifty-fifty chances of making it, the air around me changed. I felt a breeze. The bastards were right behind me. I dared not look. Slowing my run by turning around was a death sentence.

Lights up ahead! The doctor's camp! Light started filling my path. My chances were seventy-five-twenty-five.

Bugs landed on me. Death's cold hand started to grip my balls.

In desperation, I hurled myself into the camp. Orange, searing flames covered the sky above me. I heard the scorching and dropping of insects to the ground.

Looking up, I met the Doofer Brothers for the first time.

Chapter 16

THE DOOFER BROTHERS

The Doofer Brothers looked alike and shared the same last name but were not related. One was named Sam; the other, Samuel. Both were overweight and possessed a dirty vernacular.

Their ability to build improvised death devices was beyond reproach. Their skill was amazing. That morning, they'd rigged some propane tanks to metal water sprayers. After suffering similar insect problems as mine, they devised this ingenious and effective solution to the bugs. Lighting the sprayers as the dawn broke, they created a flame so strong, the bugs fled back to hell.

Even though I owed them my life, I never said as much. Giving them more than a "Thank you," invited their bragging. Bragging was how men like these two dealt with compliments. They never learned how to take a compliment. They knew little about civilized life.

They scared the hell out of me. They were large hairy men with the advantages of weapons and higher ground. Provoking a confrontation with them was the last thing on my mind. My face wore an expression of meekness and confusion. After they shot a flaming inferno over my head and incinerated the small flying bugs which followed me here, I now offered them my hand as much for assistance as a gesture of goodwill.

They greeted me with a shotgun barrel to my face.

Sam said, "You think this one's sick, Samuel?"

Samuel said, "I don't know. Bugs still chase him if he was?"

Sam said, "Probably not."

Samuel said, "Who is he?"

Sam asked me, "You heard him. Who are you?"

That was a good question. For the past month, I'd wondered who I was. A college student? A friend? A murderer?

I said, "I am a bug killer."

They looked at each other and then back down at me.

Sam said, "That works for me."

Samuel said, "Works for me too."

Fraternity life had taught me much about the male condition, especially in matters of life and death. Fraternity social norms won the day with other primitive males in only a few words.

I said, "You two going to keep standing there, or you going to help me up?"

Sam offered me his hand. When I gripped it, he did more than pull me up. He threw me through the air. By putting one foot out in front of me, I kept myself from falling again on my face. The bastard didn't know his own strength.

Samuel said, "What are you doing out here? Killing bugs?"

I said, "They attacked my friend and me. He wasn't so lucky. I've been running since."

I left out any mention of sacrificing our girlfriend or my friend killing himself. I lied about everything. When surrounded by dumb people, it's best to play dumb.

I said, "What y'all doing out here?"

They looked at each other. For a while, they didn't say anything. They faced each other and made faces without speaking. Between them, there existed a redneck, psychic link.

Sam said, "That's for us to know."

I said, "Have you heard about Dr. Joyce out here?"

They stopped.

Samuel said, "What exactly are you doing out here?"

I said, "Do you know her?"

I didn't know whether these idiots worked for Dr. Joyce or whether they'd killed her. I hoped it was the former.

Samuel said, "Maybe."

I said, "I have something to show her."

Samuel said, "Show us."

I said, "I can show all of you."

While both of them brandished their firearms, Sam said, "Okay, but you walk in front of us."

I started walking in the direction he'd indicated towards with his shotgun. Not knowing if they planned on taking me to see Dr. Joyce or a death pit with her body in it, I kept my eye on the Doofer Brothers as I walked.

They took me to a large tent. Outside of it lay different kinds of digging tools and boxes of rocks. A multitude of ropes held the tent up along with a wooden beam that ran over the top. A power cord from a generator snaked its way underneath the tent and a hose dangled from a plastic water bin the size of a small pool. It looked like an expedition.

I said, "Holy crap, where's the buffet?"

Samuel walked over to the tent's opening and said into it, "Doctor, someone's here. He wants to talk with you."

My heart lifted and my stomach flipped. At last, this was the moment I waited for. My induction into the halls of happiness. Meeting Dr. Joyce promised a future full of her sunshine and warmth. She would make me complete.

I heard a loud, whiny voice come from inside the tent. "Who? Tell him to go away. I am busy."

This was not the dream meeting with the doctor I hoped for. It was shattered.

Samuel said, "He's standing right here."

I heard her say, "Ugh, okay."

She came out of the tent.

Her appearance shocked me. In my mind, Doctor Joyce was larger than life. She was a goddess. Beautiful and strong, she was my safe vessel in a harbor of chaos.

The real Doctor Joyce didn't match my version. She was diminutive. Nothing about her hinted at an underlying strength. If anything, she was fragile. Upon seeing her, one wondered how she'd survived outdoors. I felt my upper lip curl in disappointment.

Without saying a word, for dramatic effect, I took the image out of my pocket and presented it to her.

She said, "Who the hell are you and what they hell is that?"

I said, "You don't know?"

She said, "What? That stupid rock or who you are?"

I said, "The rock."

Scrunching her brow and snarling her lip, she said, "You want rocks? I have a ton of rocks. You want one?"

She walked to one of the buckets, picked up a rock and threw it at me. I turned to avoid it hitting me.

She said, "There. You want some more goddamn rocks?"

I said, "Aren't you here looking for aliens?"

She looked at me with a blank expression and then burst into laughter. After laughing for what seemed like half an hour, she said, "Where did you get that idea?"

I said, "From your website."

She scrunched her eyebrows again and then a smile spread across her lips. She said, "Oh the stuff in South America? I did that for my funding. I didn't believe in any of that. I needed the money for real research."

I said, "Well, what are you looking for?"

She said, "Tombs, actually. Old grave sites."

I said, "Well, I found this stone at the Mud Caves. It could be related?"

She said, "Okay, give it to me, little boy."

After I handed it to her, she looked it over in her hands. She said, "Interesting. Where did you find it, exactly?"

I said, "At the very bottom. Until the bugs chased us out."

She said, "Us?"

I said, "Yea, my friend wasn't so lucky with the bugs."

She said, "Yeah, we've had bug problems ourselves. Some hired hands became sick. And our horses died. We do everything with ATVs these days. The Doofers have done a good job of killing the bugs, though."

I'd witnessed her condition before. John had suffered from it. Complete denial of our present circumstances. The image infested everyone with madness. She was lucky to have two idiots who played along with her and who were great at killing things.

Somehow, I liked her. She was not the woman of my dreams but she still cut a mean frame. Her body's curves were impossible not to look at. Her high cheekbones and youth would make a lumberjack blush.

She asked, "How did you get to the bottom? That place was impossible."

I said, "I don't know for sure. My friend did. I went back outside."

She said, "Wow, what a friend you are. Come inside. Let's talk about this rock."

The inside of the tent looked like an apartment, containing a desk with a leather chair, a queen-sized cot, and a portable stove. When I imagined the Doofers carrying all of this, my back hurt.

She sat at her desk, and I joined her using a fold out chair. She said she chose the Smoky Mountains after seeing some television shows

75

about the place. Selling her work to donors was easy with popular TV topics.

She showed me a map with all her sites on the internet. She picked each site based on geographical features such as caves, except for her current location.

After she'd hired the Doofer brothers, they told her about their current location. How the locals always avoided this place. They said too, that recently it had started getting weirder. Hearing this, she'd rented a ground-penetrating radar to go over the land. In doing so, they found cavernous pockets underground.

They planned on using an auger to drill this location for access to the caves. The Doofers set up an auger a few hundred yards from her tent, on the edge of one of the subterranean caverns.

She said, "So, I've told you about me. Tell me about you."

I told her about researching the image in Japan. How finding its image on a rock over here changed the course of history.

She laughed and said, "Listen, the researchers in Japan were just yanking your chain. That rock is probably nothing. Researchers will say anything to get paid."

I said, "Aren't you worried about the bugs? They chased me all the way here."

She said, "What? A few little bugs? You make them sound like an army. Until now, we haven't seen them since we started setting up the drill."

The last part was interesting. Why did the bugs stop coming here? Did they want her to drill?

I said, "Do you think it's okay for me to hang out for the drilling?"

She said, "You have your own camping gear?"

I said, "Yes."

She said, "Sure, just don't get in my way."

"I won't."

I wasn't so sure about this. I came here looking for someone to save me. My conversation with the doctor convinced me she needed more saving than me.

When I walked out the tent, Sam said, "Don't talk to her about the bugs."

I said, "Hey, I was meaning to ask you, what do you guys do with the ones who get infected?"

Upon hearing this, Sam glared at me and walked away. Just like me, he worried about possible murder charges. Being careful around the Doofers was a must. I didn't want to end up like one of the "infected".

That night, as we prepared for sleep, the Doofers put up canvas walls and assembled the largest bug zapper in recorded history. Using several solar generators, metal poles and chicken wire, they stretched a metal roof over our heads with thousands of volts running through it. I didn't know if the zapper killed humans, but I was not going to find out.

Underneath this wired monstrosity of electrocution, they set up a failsafe. After hauling in space heaters with funnels on top, they connected all their ignition switches to a remote. If the electricity failed, their next plan was unleashing the fires of heaven.

I did not ask them what would happen if the chicken wire ignited a funnel; or why they didn't just put up a canvas ceiling as well. Understanding the Doofers meant not asking questions. Questions made them angry.

When we rolled out our sleeping bags, I said, "Hey, Sam and Samuel, I have a surprise for you."

From my backpack I produced a ten-pound bag of DDT, threw it at Sam, and said, "You can add this to your arsenal."

After this sign of professional courtesy, we all slept well that night.

Chapter 17

THE AUGER

Our sleep was peaceful. I didn't like it. Without bugs crawling up my ass, things were strange.

Drilling into the caverns was a bad idea. Last time I went into a hole like that around here, my best friend's leg came flying out, with the shoe still on it.

The Doofers didn't take no for an answer. They didn't like any answers. It was their way or a double barrel shotgun to your face.

For the auger, they brought metal tubing and an industrial endoscope with thermal imaging. Once they drilled to the cavern, they planned on inserting the tubing in the hole. With the tubing in place, managing the endoscope was easy.

Dr. Joyce didn't concern herself with any of the drilling. She deferred to the Doofers. How hard was it drilling a hole?

The Doofers were different. They knew what faced them. While Dr. Joyce deluded herself and focused on her work, the Doofers planned their next attack. They refused to accept defeat. When it came to death and destruction, they rose to the occasion.

They charged their bug zapper and placed their space heaters. They readied their guns. They took the DDT I gave them and strapped dynamite to it.

I didn't understand their ultimate goal. Exploding the dynamite made the DDT inert. But I never questioned them. Refusing to do what the Doofers said was not an option. Crossing them in the middle of nowhere was a death wish. Staying on their good side was staying alive.

The drilling took the whole day. Due to the length of the hole, the dig was not simple. Using water to improve the digging and clearing the auger were mandatory. The work was hard and time-consuming.

Late in the afternoon the auger lurched forward and breached the cavern. After we pulled out the auger and inserted tubing, we snaked the endoscopy down the hole to take a peek.

The hole was long and deep. It took several minutes to lower the camera down. At the bottom of the hole, we switched on the thermal imaging. Sand covered the cavern floor. Not anticipating soft terrain, we submerged our camera in the sand. After wiggling free of the sand, the thermal scanned the room.

By pure luck, our drilling resulted in a discovery. Even though the cavern was huge, the auger uncovered a small room. As the camera moved around, it showed a chamber with one exit and an altar.

As we moved the camera closer, we made out the details of the altar. Chiseled into the wall were insects, supporting a shelf. On this shelf in high relief was the image on my stone.

I whispered, "She Who Shall Not Be Named."

Hearing me, Sam said, "Shut the hell up with that mumbo jumbo."

The sun sank in the evening sky. Exhausted from the effort of the day, we pulled the camera up. We agreed to search more in the morning.

As Samuel put the endoscopy back in its case, the ground rumbled. Buzzing filled my ears and I fell to my knees.

Sam said, "What's that rumbling and what the hell are you doing on your knees?"

The auger pipe started shaking. It intensified in rhythm. Over its noise, Samuel yelled, "Whatever's down there is coming up!"

The first one that came out was large. A flying bug the size of a small dog exited the tube. The luminescence in its carapace lit up everything around it. Its body was a composition of gross, neon-rainbow color and short, greasy hairs. It was enough fuel for instant insanity, and its hideous face trumped it. The small wings buzzed at a furious pace and moaned under the weight of its body.

As it lifted its body up into the air, it revealed the visage underneath. In its undercarriage hung the plump face of a black-eyed newborn baby.

Sam said, "What in the hell?"

No sooner did the words leave his mouth than Sam helped me up and we all ran for the bug zapper. Dozens of the bugs followed us.

While we stood underneath the zapper, the insects suicided themselves on it. Flying into it hard and fast, the impact of their bodies sounded like drums. Sticking on the wire even after death, they sparked and smoked.

Samuel yelled, "Sam, we have to shut the breach!"

After tossing the improvised DDT explosive in Sam's direction, Samuel fired up two hand-held chainsaws and went running towards the auger. With Sam close on his heels, he hacked and slashed the bug bodies in his way.

Upon arriving at the auger, Sam lit the dynamite and yelled, "Fire in the hole!" and threw the DDT and dynamite into the hole.

Homing in on the zapper's electrical charge, the bugs continued their self-destructive onslaught on its wires. When the Doofers returned to the zapper's electrical umbrella, we all braced ourselves for the explosion. Over the sound of the electrocuted bugs, Samuel yelled, "When it goes off, let's hope our zapper doesn't go down!"

When the dynamite exploded, I realized how giving them the DDT was a mistake. Not only did the auger hole collapse, but the whole cavern exploded, burying it under tons of earth. Under such an explosion nothing lived. Even if it wasn't inert, using the DDT was overkill.

Although the ground shook, the wire and space heaters held firm. Samuel pulled out his remote and ignited the space heaters, sending their fires straight up and torching the remaining insects. A stench like raw eggs accompanied the falling bug bodies. The smoldering insects set our tents and equipment on fire. Before we knew it, a huge blaze started.

Samuel yelled, "Screw it! We need to get to the ATVs and split!"

Grabbing as much gear as possible, we jumped on the ATVs. There were three. One was meant for Dr. Joyce, but she rode on Sam's backseat. I took the third.

As we rode like bats out of hell away from the fires, I yelled, "Yeeeee Aaaawwww! See you in hell, bug bastards!"

Stopping our vehicles at a summit overlooking the valley and its clearing, Samuel said, "The sun's going down; we need to make camp somewhere before we ride into a tree."

Sam said, "Well, that puts us in a pickle. We don't have any tents, and most of our supplies are gone."

I said, "Those things will come back. I guarantee it."

Samuel said, "Well, Mr. Genius. Any thoughts on where we can go? Our trucks are more than a day's travel from here to Tennessee."

I said, "My truck's closer. There are some buildings on the way. They look empty,. but, I did hear chanting when I camped there."

Samuel said, "Well, let's go have a look."

As we drove off into the falling night, I wondered how I'd met new people even though I was surrounded by destruction. Didn't people smell death on me?

Chapter 18

THE CULT OF BUGS

My drone was lost in the great fire. Without it, inspecting the abandoned buildings was impossible. Driving down to the buildings on our ATVs was our only option.

The early evening sky glistening off their tanks, our ATVs hummed down the hill to the old village. With their silhouettes blacking out the sky, they looked like messengers from a black hell.

With one hand on the steering, I fingered my .45. With the ability to stop a man at fifty yards, my sidearm was sexy. If our ATVs were the messenger, my .45 was the message.

About twenty yards out, we stopped the ATVs. Reaching down and warming his hands on the engine, Samuel said, "Well, who's going first?"

Sam said, "I will," and popping a wheelie, headed down the hill.

That goddamn village. Even in the night, its walls were bright white, like some damnable power gave it energy. Its facades made an uneven frown in the night. As the moon started to spill its light over it, the town opened its fractured smile and swallowed it.

We waited for Sam. If he returned, great. If he gave us a signal, just as good. If neither happened, Samuel and I knew burning the village to the ground was our best option. Its buildings provided ample fuel for a great campfire.

We saw the headlight of his ATV returning. As its beams bounced off the dilapidated houses, the headlight acted as a cinemascope looking into a hell made of shadows.

Tapping my sidearm, I noticed the ATV still possessed a rider. Looking closer, I confirmed that an alive Sam rode it.

He drove up to us, "Well, one building has its lights on."

Samuel said, "Which one?"

Sam said, "The church."

The church was at the end of the street. Hanging over our bikes like oversized grave markers, the buildings looked down on us like silent witnesses to an execution. There was no movement inside them. As the moon's rays illuminated their windows, the buildings pleaded for us to release the evil within.

We drove slowly. We rode our ATVs like bad asses taking their time to go to hell. Of our group, only Dr. Joyce and I bothered looking around. Sam and Samuel fixed their gaze straight ahead at the church.

The church appeared normal. Its facade consisted of a bell tower with an oversized window and a steeple. Light illuminated the outline of its double doors. The light didn't go far beyond the church's threshold. It retreated from the night.

We pulled our bikes up alongside each other, forming a line. We dismounted our bikes in sync and walked to the church steps.

Samuel walked up the steps and knocked on one of the doors.

Both doors flung open. A little old man stood there. He wore a huge smile and said, "Welcome."

Samuel said, "Greetings. Are you taking visitors?"

The preacher said, "Sure, come on in," and stepped aside for us.

Samuel nodded to the rest of us, and we walked up the stairs. The church smelled like old socks. Its interior was sparse with a few pews and a decrepit pulpit.

Samuel said, "You still have services here, Father?"

The preacher said, "We still do. On Sundays."

Samuel said, "How big's the turnout?"

The preacher said, "I don't draw many these days. But I do okay."

Samuel said, "What happened to this place?"

The preacher said, "It's an old lumber town. When mills started in Tennessee most everybody moved there. I stayed here."

Samuel said, "Why did you stay? Why not open a church there?"

The preacher said, "This is my church, here."

Everything made too much goddamn sense. I didn't like it. The sooner we left this place the better.

Samuel said, "Mind if we stay a bit, preacher?"

The preacher said, "Sure. All are welcome in the house of God."

Great.

I asked, "You have a toilet?"

Both Dr. Joyce and I went to the lavatory which was located next to the vestry. Dr. Joyce used it first.

When I walked back to the nave, Dr. Joyce and Samuel talked to the preacher. Sam sat off to the side. I perched next to him.

Sam said, "So, what's with the 'She Who Shall Not Be Named' stuff?"

I said, "It's what someone called them in New Mexico."

He said, "What happened to them?"

I said, "He died, I think."

He said, "Holy crap, man. Anyone else who died that you didn't tell us about?"

I said, "Well, since we're in a church, I will tell you. There were several."

He said, "Crap! How many?"

I said, "To be honest, I lost count."

He said, "How about your friend?"

I said, "Yeah, he died. My other friend too."

He said, "You're a regular slaughterhouse. Anything else you are not telling us? You kill anyone?"

I said, "I shot a few. And I set a fire that killed some."

He said, "Goddamn murdering arsonist."

I said, "How about you and Samuel. Kill anyone lately?"

He looked at me and said, "Yeah, we had some trouble with some of Dr. Joyce's helpers. Their heads turned into honeycombs."

He gestured around his head with movements meant to look like bugs flying. This guy was a real psycho-killer nut-job.

I said, "Sorry, I asked."

"Don't worry about it."

I said, "Thanks."

Staying in the Doofers' good graces was a must. They didn't flinch when taking someone out. I fancied making myself number one on their list of likes.

The preacher said, "Are you hungry?"

Samuel said, "Sure."

When the preacher left, Samuel asked us, "So what do you guys think?"

I said, "This place sucks."

This place did suck. It smelled of mold. Although the pews, stage and altar were a faded white, the floors and ceiling were made of old, yellow pine. A place like this creaked all the time. With a strong wind, it could fall down. The only thing comforting about it was the mysterious lack of spider webs.

He said, "Shut the hell up. Anyone else?"

Dr. Joyce said, "This is probably not a good time, but I'm going to need to tell my donors we had complications. Might be a while before we can come back."

Dr. Joyce was nuts. Even after witnessing the fourth horseman of the apocalypse, she worried about her research. Her intentions were noble to a fault.

He said, "That's okay, Doctor. We can worry about that later. Let's try to stay here until morning comes."

When the preacher came back, there were two people with him, holding trays of cookies. He said, "These are a couple of my parishioners. Eddy and Anna."

The cookies looked stale. The two people reminded me of the elders in the mad town.

Samuel said, "Nice to meet you all."

The preacher said, "After cookies, we will have service."

No one ate the cookies. They were not the most appetizing. In light of recent events, people lacked an appetite.

I tried talking to Eddy. "So you live here in town?"

He said, "No."

This was going great. I said, "Well, you live close by?"

He said, "We talk later. After service."

Oh man, I heard a few idiots talk like this before in the mad town. I said, "Oh, okay."

The preacher walked to the pulpit. Eddy and Anna sat in the front row. The preacher began. "Moses said that the locusts will cover the land and eat everything that is to be eaten. But who are the locusts?"

We all looked at each other.

He continued, "Like little bugs, we swarm this planet. Eating off God's creation. Destroying it. We don't know peace. We have a big hole in place of the holy spirit. All we know is how to keep devouring. With no worry about our immortal spirit. Until now, that is."

He stepped back from the podium and opened his robes. To our horror, his legs were just tibia. A honeycomb of insects lived in his chest. In their little cells, they lived little insect lives, hatching larvae.

He said in a soft voice, "Don't worry, friends. I was scared at first too. But I accepted them, and they gave me peace. They turned me into God's creation."

He started chanting. Eddy and Anna joined in.

The buzzing blasted me again. Grabbing my head with both hands and squeezing hard seemed the only thing to do.

Samuel stood up and cocked his shotgun. He said, "Stop this crap right now or I will start shooting."

They kept chanting. I thought, "Surely, Samuel's first shot will be a warning shot."

Wrong, he blew Anna's head clean off. Her head exploded in a cloud of dust. The Doofers were stone cold killers after all.

The chanting stopped. The priest smiled, looked Samuel's way and unleashed the insects from his chest. They swarmed around Samuel's head.

Thinking Samuel the toughest of us all, I was shocked when he started screaming in a high- pitched tone and waving his arms around his head. I hope when it's my time to go, I'll go with more grace than that pussy.

Sam cried, "Samuel! Brother!"

Samuel fell to his knees with his head down. He became quiet.

Sam said, "Are you okay, Samuel?"

Samuel lifted his head, pulled out his hand-held chainsaw and said, "Time you die."

Accepting what he and his brother were and what became of his brother, Sam said, "Not if I get you first," and pulled out his chainsaw.

What ensued was the most epic chainsaw battle of all time. When their chainsaws collided, they both recoiled from the strike. As they positioned themselves for a riposte, the sound and sparks of their chainsaws stayed in the air.

The bugs were not the most adept in the art of chainsaws. They'd never studied them like the Doofers. Samuel's bug-infested brain grew confused. The confusion could be seen in his movements. He slipped.

Without hesitation or even a farewell speech, Sam drove the chainsaw into his brother's face. While Dr. Joyce and I looked on with shocked faces, he leapt to the pulpit and knocked down the preacher.

Chopping off one of the preacher's tibiae, he said, "Now hop around you, insect bastard."

When the preacher attempted to respond, Sam ended it. While turning towards Eddy, Sam's chainsaw died. He pulled out his gun and finished off Eddy, exploding his head into a dust cloud.

I said, "Wow, that was epic."

He said, "You stupid piece of crap. This is all you. None of this would have happened if you hadn't brought those bugs to us."

Seeing him point the gun at me, I raised my hands. "Hey, you guys blew up the cave. I'm just as much a victim in this as you guys."

He said, "It still might feel good to kill you."

I said, "In front of Dr. Joyce? That wouldn't be professional."

He looked at her and then back to me. He said, "You're lucky she's her and that I'm a professional and all that."

With blood, brain dust and dead bugs everywhere, Dr. Joyce's sanity was on the brink. Her eyes twitched. Her hands shook. She mumbled.

Even in her ruined state, Dr. Joyce retained some of the features which attracted her to me. Her high cheek bones and educated airs put her above me, but I still felt sorry for her. The poor lady. I saw her as my savior and sought freedom in her arms. By coming here, I'd poisoned her sanity. If she lost her mind, the blame was mine.

I offered her my hand. I said, "Things will be okay."

We headed for the door. Opening it and looking outside, we saw the entire remaining congregation. There were no less than twenty insect deformities staring back at us. Fiends with antennae, tibia, and thorax stood there. I slammed the door and said, "Not that way."

Holding Dr. Joyce's hand, I said, "Let's make for the back."

Sam said, "What about our bikes?"

I said, "Forget them, unless you want to end up like one of those things."

He said, "Screw you, I'm getting out of here," and he opened the doors and ran out.

While Sam distracted the bugs, I ran with Dr. Joyce to the vestry, where I'd seen a window earlier. After I opened the window and helped Dr. Joyce out, I jumped out myself. Behind the church was about fifty yards of open land and then a drop into the forest. Hoping the drop wasn't steep, we ran for it.

The drop wasn't straight. It sloped a little. It wasn't very high either. I lowered Dr. Joyce and jumped down myself. We ran into the forest, out of view of the church.

Running as fast as possible through the forest at night, we didn't look back. We ran and ran until we arrived at a small stream. We both bent down to drink a little.

Dr. Joyce said, "Look, you can see the church."

Turning my head in the direction of her voice, I saw the silhouette of the church in the distance. Since our current location was below it, the church looked like it was on a cliff.

As I looked closer, a grim detail stood out to me. On the top of its spire, there was no cross. A body hung there. I knew who it was. The fat torso and small head belonged to Sam.

Ignoring the pale body reflected in the moonlight at the top of the church, I said, "Well, that sure is tasty water. We better keep moving."

By luck, my compass was intact. Using it and the stars, we made our way to my truck. John's keys were in my pocket.

Judging by the hours traveled, the SUV was close. An hour from our current location was a good estimate.

Dr. Joyce said, "You hear that?"

Her paranoia made her senses hyper-aware. I listened closer. Footfalls sounded around us.

I whispered, "Listen. This is what we're going to do. I'm going to distract them. And you will use my compass and head south."

She said, "But you will die."

I said, "Yeah, but I probably deserve it. And I've had a crush on you for a long time."

She looked at me and ran off.

Well, that's one way to motivate a woman to run.

I yelled, "Hey, buggers! Come and get me. My brain tastes good! Come and honeycomb me!"

In the pale light of the moon, their dark outlines assembled. All sorts of perversions stood around me. They made no sound or movement. They wanted to wait, but I didn't.

Unholstering my .45, I emptied my clip in the bodies standing south of me. A .45 is called a man stopper for a reason. Those bastards flew far. Even if they lived somehow, they were out of my way.

I ran after Dr. Joyce. While in stride, I reloaded my gun with another clip. I sprinted a few yards, turned and unloaded the entirety of the new clip. I saw several bodies fly.

I ran hard. Conserving as much breath and energy as possible, my running form was tight and focused. To catch me, those insect bastards better have the lung capacity of an Olympic runner!

Up ahead, I saw the treeline and then the SUV sitting there in the moonlight. Getting closer, I couldn't see Dr. Joyce.

She was late, lost or food. Since the bugs were not on me yet, I took the time to start the truck and point it towards the treeline. When the time came, I planned on turning on the lights to blind the bugs.

Lowering the driver's seat window and opening the door, I took up position with my firearm pointing towards the tree line, resting my arms on the windowsill of the car door.

After waiting for a few minutes, Dr. Joyce came into view.

I started shouting, "Over here! Over here!"

Following the sound of my voice she looked up and ran towards me. She ran fast. She looked stressed. Tears streamed down her cheeks.

I yelled, "You can make it! You are doing great!"

When she made it to the parking area, I said, "Get in the truck." I didn't take my eyes off the forest for a minute.

As soon as she opened the door and sat down, the insects appeared in the trees. By turning on the lights of the SUV and firing my .45, the bugs scattered.

I jumped in the truck and hauled ass. Putting the Smoky Mountains in my rear view, my journey ended.

As I Looked over at Dr. Joyce, she looked back at me with a weird smile and huge eyes. Her journey was not over yet.

We drove back to the bed and breakfast in Hendersonville. Since we'd already pre-paid for the week, I took Dr. Joyce straight to our rooms.

Seeing John's unopened bags shocked me. Reminding me of better days, their presence drained me emotionally. Putting them in the dumpster outside the hotel gave me peace of mind.

Dr. Joyce was out of sorts. She didn't talk. She didn't blink. Her eyes were crazed. She jerked her head around like she could see something unseen. She was a nut.

The first night, I put my bedding on the floor in front of her bed. Neither one of us slept. We both felt those bastards pursuing us. As nightfall crept into the room, the window became a dark portal for the bug invasion. Every creek of the floorboards was their army ascending the stairs to enter our room.

The bugs wanted us. They meant to get us. Although more than a hundred miles separated us from the Smoky Mountains, leaving this hellhole dominated my mind. Visions of cruel bugs eating us chilled the blood in my veins. How long do they live in bodies? Are the hosts aware? Did one of the bugs go up Dr. Joyce's nose?

The second night, we slept. Our rest was needed. Both of us faced emotional and physical collapse. Consisting of my hazing days at the fraternity, my dreams were happy and joyous.

Something woke me. While my eyes popped open with shock and awe, my ears listened for anything foreign. An invader.

In the street below our window, a trash can lid fell to the ground. Footsteps followed the noise. Reluctant to make my presence known at the window, my body moved slowly to it. Looking down from one side of the window, my eyes spied movement in the street. Weird, dark movement. Did I see something with spider legs? Or the head of a mantis? Was I becoming a nut like Dr. Joyce?

The next morning, my mind was made up. We needed to get the hell out of there. Whether a real emergency or an abundance of caution, the reason mattered little. Hanging around in this small town invited trouble.

Convincing Dr. Joyce of this was another matter. Convincing her of anything was a problem. For all I knew, she still thought we were in the Smoky Mountains.

I said, "You want to see your family, Doctor?"

She said, "Family?"

I said, "Yes, they're probably worried sick about you. I know I would be."

She said, "Yes, family."

I said, "You want to see them, right? Family?"

She said, "Yes. See. Yes."

Grabbing her driver's license, I looked up her address on the internet. It was an apartment. Probably not her parents' place.

Since I was fresh out of other addresses, I pointed at her driver's license and said, "Let's go here. Okay?"

She said, "Yes, go there."

Using her credit card to buy her ticket and John's card to buy mine, I put us on a flight out of Asheville bound for New York. The drive there was a few hours but there were still several hours of daylight. Taking off before the sun rose was doable.

After packing both mine and Dr. Joyce's bag, the only hard part came in convincing Dr. Joyce to get out of bed. In the past two days, once or twice she'd risen to use the bathroom but that was it.

I said, "Hey, Doctor, don't you want to go home and sleep in your bed? It's nicer! Warmer!"

Cradling my hands under her head and legs, I pulled her out of bed. Sitting her on the couch, I dressed her. I didn't change her underwear. I only put clothes over her, tied her shoes, brushed her hair, and tried pulling her to her feet.

When I grabbed both her hands to pull her up, she let her fingers slip through mine. She fell back on the couch and curled up in a fetal position.

I said, "You'll be okay."

I put my arms underneath her again and carried her to the SUV. I let her lie down in the back seat.

Our return to Asheville surprised me. Without any bugs or hysterics, our drive was pleasant. It calmed me.

After merging over a couple of lanes and taking the return exit, we arrived at our car rental location. Everything was easy, except getting Dr. Joyce out of the SUV. After opening the door and grabbing her feet, I slid her into a wheelchair borrowed from the rental place.

When I loaded her onto the lift bus, I stood with her as the gate went up. Fastening her to one of the wheelchair seats, I made sure she was safe.

As I sat down next to her, I put my arm around her and looked out the window. One of the workers drove our SUV to the car wash facility. The SUV was dirty from sitting in the parking lot for weeks.

I smiled to myself that the trip was over. When the bus headed out and I turned my head to look in front of me, something caught my eye. In the undercarriage of the SUV hung a hive. The bugs flew around it. They tracked us! My chest tightened, and I swallowed hard.

Despite my racing heart, I dared not show Dr. Joyce what I'd seen. If she thought for a second that we were in trouble, getting her on the plane would be next to impossible.

Checking in and running to our gate became a priority. The workers at the check-in counter thankfully didn't inquire into Dr. Joyce's condition. They seemed quite understanding and sympathetic.

When the plane's wheels went up and the plane soared into the air, a sigh of relief left my lips. The only thing left to worry about were the bugs attaching themselves to our plane.

Chapter 19

DR. JOYCE'S PLACE

When the plane landed, I wheeled Dr. Joyce to the baggage terminal and then to a cab stand outside. After hailing a cab and giving the driver Dr. Joyce's address, I lifted her into the cab.

With the window cracked, the cool fall air wafted through the cab. Lining the highway, the trees were a vibrant green against the black night. My soul felt free.

My desire for adventure was dead. Following John to New Mexico and then the Smoky Mountains had been the worst ideas of my life. As those travels had led to Joy's and then John's death, they were even worse decisions for them. My regrets were a luxury compared to their fates.

My chance for redemption was helping Dr. Joyce. Blame for her predicament fell on me. My dishonesty had contributed to her insanity. One friend eaten alive, and the other's leg blown out of a cave were important facts to tell her. Their omission was the worst form of lying. Helping her now was my way out of my self-loathing.

Basically, I was the kiss of death. I avoided any kind of responsibility and gleefully followed my friends down their pathway to hell.

Our car pulled into the driveway leading to her apartment. Dr. Joyce's building was a brownstone surrounded by maples. It was close to the university where she worked.

After the car dropped us off at the building's entrance, I left our luggage on the sidewalk and carried Dr. Joyce into the elevator. Once we'd made it to her apartment, I fumbled for her keys and opened the door.

Her apartment was too big for one person. After laying her down on her bed and sitting on the corner of it, I scanned the bedroom for pictures. There were none.

No evidence of a boyfriend. This at least took away my worry of being killed by a jealous university student or teacher. Although my search of the whole apartment did yield pictures, these pictures were family photos. They lacked any kind of lover's intimacy.

Sitting in her living room with the lights off, I deliberated on my role in these events. I imagined living in this apartment and having some moron bringing my vegetative body back here. I hoped her family was nice.

In her pictures, her family was big with what looked to be six siblings. By my count, there were three brothers and three sisters. Believing all of them were patient and compassionate was wishful thinking at best.

I focused on her brothers. They looked gnarly. If I were one of them, engaging in a rational conversation with someone like me would be a joke. A punch to the face was more likely. I licked my front teeth. I did not want them to disappear from my mouth.

After I pulled out my phone and surfed the internet, my plan came to fruition. Dr. Joyce's university provided mental health services to their teachers and students. Assuming she obtained her funding through the university, entering her in their psych ward was plausible. Once she became a patient there, talking to her sisters about her condition would be more practical.

I laid myself out on her couch and stared at her family picture. I fell asleep. I dreamed.

I walked on ice with mounds of sand all over. I heard buzzing, but it was low and soothing. I looked up. A huge bug towered over me. I heard it say in a woman's voice, "It is your destiny to join me. You will know peace."

I woke up. Standing over me at the foot of the couch was Dr. Joyce. She looked down on me.

I said, "Oh. Hi, Dr. Joyce. Feeling better?"

She said nothing.

I stood up. Taking her by the arm, I walked her back to her bedroom. Poor thing was sleep walking. Taking her to the mental hospital the next morning was my number one priority.

I walked over to the large double windows overlooking the forest behind her apartment building. So relaxing and soothing. I fell into a trance. For the briefest of moments, I imagined a large black aphid taking up the entire sky. I gasped and stepped back. It was gone.

We were all a little crazy, with bugs on our minds.

Chapter 20

THE UNIT

After using an application on my phone to call a car, I picked up Dr. Joyce and took her downstairs. I propped her up against me as we waited for the car outside on the bench.

When the car pulled up and the driver opened the door, I laid her down on the backseat. After putting a jacket on my lap, I rested her head on it.

As my fingers stroked her hair, its volume overwhelmed my fingers. It coiled around them like the tentacles of some great beast. A woman with such thick, beautiful hair demanded respect. For such a woman to lack the power to sit or stand up was a crime against nature. A crime against the world.

I wondered about her parents. They were not in her pictures. Were they alive? Did they stroke her hair like I did when she was a child?

Driving down the long, asphalt driveway leading to the sanitarium gave me time to think about its history. Originally, it had served as a hospital for the sick during the influenza epidemic. Afterwards, it housed the unfortunate for work farms. Eventually, after the university moved in, it became the hospital and psychiatric ward for the school of medicine.

Its facade of decaying gothic architecture made it look like a lost castle from the shadow world. Its appearance made people believe it housed dark spirits, but not me. To me, it was a psych unit.

To me, sanitariums stank of medications, soiled beds and lobotomies. The spirits they housed were those of the infirm and unwanted children. Upon seeing them, fear was a good reaction, but disgust was better.

I didn't enjoy taking Dr. Joyce here. My whole being screamed against it. My options in helping someone who had lost their mind were limited. Up to now, all my choices lead to someone's death. Now was the time for a professional to make a decision for this poor lady in my arms.

After the car dropped us off, an intern loaned us a wheelchair. We wheeled it to the intake center and requested an interview.

The place was cleaner than I'd imagined. Even though the halls smelled like bleach, its interior lacked any signs of human struggle. There was no vomit, blood or brains anywhere.

When we sat down in the consultation room, I expected a bespeckled, bald man, but a young psychiatrist greeted us instead. Although she was close to my age, she exuded professionalism and experience. Not once did she seem rattled or surprised by our presence there.

I told her all sorts of lies. I told her my name was John. I said that I worked for Dr. Joyce, and she'd become ill while investigating the Smoky Mountains. I said that she first stopped eating for some unknown reason and then she no longer left her tent.

She said, "What were you doing in the Smoky Mountains?"

I said, "Dr. Joyce is a researcher for your university. She was looking for old burial sites."

She said, "I take it you are not family?"

I said, "No, I'm not."

She said, "Do you know the names of any of her family members?"

I said, "No, I don't."

She said, "Okay, this is what's going to happen. First, I will need you to leave the room while I interview her. You can wait in the hall. If we decide to take her in, I will check her information on file with the university and notify her next of kin."

"Thanks!"

As I waited in a chair in the hallway, a worrisome realization came across my mind. What if Dr. Joyce was only catatonic around me? What if I was her trigger? What if she told the psychiatrist everything that happened?

I sighed. I didn't do anything bad in front of her. The Doofers did all the violence. They traumatized everyone.

After waiting an hour, the psychiatrist reappeared through a different door down the hall.

She said, "We have decided to take her in. I've called her sister and let her know the situation."

I said, "What's going on with her?"

She said, "Unfortunately, I can't discuss that with you. But you did the right thing bringing her here."

I said, "Which sister is coming?"

She said, "Sara."

I didn't know her siblings' names, but I did know how many of each Dr. Joyce had. Getting one of their names was a great accomplishment for me.

If Dr. Joyce had told her anything, the psychiatrist's face didn't betray it. Her composure remained rudimentary, as if Dr. Joyce's interview was typical for a day in the psych unit.

Dr. Joyce's treatment required learning how to talk again and telling the psychiatrist about what happened to her. Planning my departure around her recovery was a no brainer. Assuming a fake identity to steal my best friend's funds and staying in Dr. Joyce's place rent free were both great ways to land in jail. Blowing town without Dr. Joyce's family finding out my scam was a priority.

I gave the psychiatrist my phone number and told her to call me if anything came up. She put my number in her phone and told me the visiting hours for Dr. Joyce.

Calling a car as I walked down the hall, I let out a long breath. I wanted to leave the psych unit. Dr. Joyce's place promised rest and relaxation. It promised sanctuary from the craziness of my life.

After all my lies, I needed time to think. Sorting them from the truth became hard. Distracting my brain with lies also increased my anxiety. My lies weighed on me. They enveloped my mind like an ever-present shadow.

Honesty is the best policy. Even when you are guilty, lies make everything worse.

Chapter 21

SARA JOYCE

After I woke up in Doctor Joyce's apartment, I took a shower, changed my clothes, and put my luggage under her bed. I unlocked the bedroom window leading to a fire escape. If her family decided to check on her apartment, my plan was to bail out the window.

In one of the kitchen drawers, I found a spare key. With the spare key in my possession, giving the original key to her family was not a problem. Living in her apartment without anyone knowing became easier.

Even though I planned to leave this town in a few days, my true fate was undetermined. The bugs were a curse. Their swarm cast a darkness over my entire life and future. A constant retreat from their menace was my new normal.

John's money and credit cards were important to me now more than ever. Without his fat wallet, my ability to escape a surprise set of circumstances would be limited. His money was key to my survival. I had to make it last as long as possible.

After I fixed myself some soup, I sat down at the kitchen table and looked out the double windows. A group of storm clouds in the distance rolled their way to me. Imagining them as a huge swarm of insects, they looked like Armageddon.

I said out loud with no one to hear me, "Well, that's it. Better go to the psych unit."

After washing the dishes and drying them off and putting them back where I found them, I took a quick leak and headed out. Hailing a car on my phone, I jumped on the elevator and stepped off in a lobby thick with moisture. I smelled a storm coming.

Once in the car, I looked out the rear window as the car sped down the driveway. Watching the storm clouds, I wondered if outrunning a bug swarm that big was possible. If they caught up with us, what death awaited me? Would they devour, possess or transform me?

I alone understood Dr. Joyce's insanity. She wasn't scared of a bunch of bugs. She was horrified by the unseen hand that wielded them. Some forgotten goddess had now awoke to remind us how small we were. How puny our lifetimes were compared to the eons of earth's existence. This goddess promised an early retirement for the human race. A party the universe laughed at attending.

She Who Shall Not Be Named.

I don't mention these words out loud. I barely think of them. Something about them rings true. Some primordial instinct like the movement of a snake which awakens fears long forgotten. Even after millions of years of evolution, they remain as much a part of me as my own DNA.

At the same time my car pulled up in front of the psych unit, another car arrived. Out of it bounced a young lady. She was ravishing. Her large red lips glistened with moisture in the afternoon sun. Her curves begged for my attention. Just thinking of them made me blush. There and then, I decided on worshiping her.

Her face was familiar. I recalled it from Dr. Joyce's pictures. She was Sara, or one of her sisters.

Wanting to know more about her, I hurried to follow her inside. Ahead of me, she bobbed down the hall towards the psychiatrist's office. She moved fast. Fast and sexy are a great combination.

She opened a door and stepped through it, closing it behind her. I trotted over. The sign on the door listed the psychiatrist's name. I sat down in a chair facing it and waited.

Although the door was a few feet away, I didn't take my eyes off of it. When it opened, the psychiatrist walked out first, followed by the Doctor's sister.

Seeing me, the psychiatrist said, "Oh, Sara, this is the young man I told you about."

I stood up.

Sara walked up to me and said, "I understand you worked with my sister and brought her here?"

I said, "Yes, my name is John."

She said, "I'm Sara. What happened in the Smoky Mountains?"

I rattled off the same story that I told the psychiatrist. Dr. Joyce had become more and more reclusive, eventually not leaving her tent. I left out the Doofers and all the killing and dying.

I said, "Oh, I almost forgot. Here are her keys."

I dropped them in Sara's palm. She looked down at them and then up to me. "Is her stuff in her apartment?"

I said, "Yes, I didn't unpack it. I left it there."

"Do you have time to help me sort through it?"

I said, "Sure."

We shared the cost of a car back to the Doctor's place. Once there, we took the elevator up to her apartment.

When Sara opened the door and walked in, I stayed back and waited for her to invite me in. By practicing restraint, I hoped to fool Sara into believing I wasn't staying there.

She said, "Well don't be shy, come on in."

"Thanks."

I took her to Dr. Joyce's bags. "Everything I was able to carry is in there. Mostly clothes and stuff."

She opened the bags and sorted the clothes, folding them in stacks on the adjacent bed. All she found was clothes. Not packing the stone from the caves was intentional. Seeing that stone again was last on my to-do list. John sacrificed his life for that piece of rock. The stupid stone took everything from me. It robbed me of my friends and their sanity. My refusal to covet it had protected me.

After she finished with the bags, Sara walked around the apartment looking things over and organizing them. She went into the kitchen and started opening and closing drawers.

She said, "Did you spend the night here?"

I blushed. I said, "Just one night."

She said, "Where are the spare keys? Do you have them?"

I froze. Looking like a liar in front of my goddess ruined the moment. I said, "Oh yeah, I have those too, sorry."

She held out her hand. The smirk on her face let me know she didn't buy any of this. It gave me the impression she no longer considered me trustworthy.

She said, "Are you trying to stay here rent free?"

After I handed the keys to her, I looked down at my feet and said, "Yes."

When I didn't look up, she put her hand on my shoulder and said, "It's all right. You can stay here a few more nights. But my sisters and brothers are going to want you to leave. We can't have you living here while we are trying to sort out my sister's life."

She grabbed my hand and put the keys into it. Her hands were warm. After touching me, their warmth spread up my arms to my whole body. Her touch made me feel safe and secure. She really was a goddess.

I said, "Thanks. I won't stay long, I promise. I need to get going as well."

My planning didn't go beyond a day. For the past months, my life had been in survival mode. Avoiding one catastrophe after another consumed all my energy. Thinking of what to do when the crisis was over never crossed my mind. Thanks to the Joyce family and my imminent departure from Dr. Joyce's flat, returning to California was my best option.

Leaving Sara was heartbreaking. Her presence purged negativity from my mind. Her beauty, charm and warmth inspired me.

For her, though, my leaving was best. Her eyes betrayed worry and concern for her sister. If she knew my whole story, I was toast.

In all the death surrounding me, my involvement was the common thread. Believe me, I didn't hold myself responsible for everything that happened. I wasn't the hand that killed my best friend and his girlfriend or drove my crush to insanity. My guilt came from association. Wherever I went, death followed me. Desiring my company was crazy. Sara asking me questions about my involvement was inevitable.

Once the shock of her sister's condition wore off, her clearer mind presented a real problem for me. Up to now, I was lucky. No one asked me any hard questions. The more time given to people like the psychiatrist and Sara to think about me, the more my oddity became apparent.

She said, "You want to get something to eat?"

We went to a local Mexican restaurant. The food paled in comparison to New Mexico's. It lacked flavor or chili. It was cheese on bread.

My last meal with someone at a restaurant preceded their death. I hoped this was not the case this time. Sara was great company. We talked and told jokes. Between gulps of tea, we laughed out loud. Everything was great until I brought up her family.

I said, "So, tell me about your brothers and sisters."

Her family's past was dark. After committing double suicide, their parents left the children enough money to fend for themselves. Understandably, none of them married in adulthood.

I said, "Oh God, I'm sorry."

She said that their lives together were difficult for many years, making the bonds between brothers and sisters strong. Dr. Joyce's illness threatened those bonds. While she was the cool headed one of the group, her brothers and sisters were more excitable. She foresaw her sister's condition taking the worry of their sibling family to dangerous levels. Levels not seen since the death of her parents.

Since Dr. Joyce's past was full of trauma, her current state was understandable. Was Dr. Joyce's past the reason why the psychiatrist and Sara didn't suspect me of wrongdoing?

I said, "How did your parents' death affect Dr. Joyce?"

She said that of all her brothers and sisters, she took it the hardest. She was the youngest and cried for weeks. They feared she lacked the strength to go on.

I said, "Care for dessert?"

I won't lie. No matter how hard I try, resisting one is impossible. Warm brownies and cookies with ice cream are best. We ordered one of each and shared them.

When we left the restaurant, she said, "Well, I'm going home. I'll give you a call tomorrow."

I said, "Sounds good. I'll stay at the Doctor's place tonight. But I'll only stay there a few nights. I promise."

She gave me a small hug and we parted ways. Watching her bounce away made me smile. Everything she did tickled me. She was spectacular. She took my mind off everything. She restored my sanity.

By all rights, I'd earned the same fate as all the others in my life up to now. I belonged dead or institutionalized. Fate kept me alive. My belief in fate also explained my dreams and the buzzing. My mind played tricks on me. My brain struggled for control of my situation, causing me to imagine these things. Or so I thought.

As I waited for a car, I looked up at the night sky. It was empty of stars. I remembered the first time we entered the mad town. Waking from my slumber in the back seat, I believed something took the stars from me.

I laughed. I deserved to live in a psych unit if I believed that.

Chapter 22

JACK JOYCE

D r. Joyce's older brother was an ass. Meeting him for the first
time was a disaster. Jack and I were the two most incompatible
people on planet earth.

I returned to the psych unit for a few reasons. Alone and bored
provided good ones but wanting to see Sara again was a better one.

I rushed to get ready in the morning. Taking a shower, brushing
my teeth, and putting on my clothes all took too long. Thinking of Sara
the moment I woke up, my memory of her kickstarted my heart and
sent my blood flowing.

Maybe my initial crush on Dr. Joyce nurtured a love for a woman
like her. Or maybe Sara was everything Dr. Joyce was not. Or maybe I
was crazy. I don't know.

Like everything up to now, I reacted the same way. I played along
and went with my gut feeling. Everything was different, yet the same.
Instead of following my friend down a hole, I followed my heart to the
woman I loved.

When I arrived at the psychiatric ward, a large, round man paced
outside. His girth was extraordinary for a man his height. He was
almost as wide as he was tall. He took big, swarthy steps and waved his
free arm around him in the air as he talked on the phone.

He was also in Dr. Joyce's pictures. From talking with Sara the night
before, I assumed this was Jack.

She'd told me some stories about him. Before their parents died,
the whole family went horseback riding. After riding all day, they
wanted to ride some more, but Jack's horse lay down. Jack was so large;
he wore his horse out.

Another time, as they played putt-putt golf, a group of boys had taunted them. From this group, two of the older boys stepped forward and pushed him. Jack knocked them both out with two shots from his right hand. Jack didn't mess around.

When Sara told me this story, she described his fist coming down on the two boys like a giant club or mallet. Once I heard that, I forever remembered him as the "hammer man".

While he was on the phone, I walked past him without saying anything. I wasn't ready for "hammer time".

Dr. Joyce looked the same when I saw her again for the first time in a few days. The psychiatrist and Sara led me into her room. As long as a family member accompanied me, they didn't have a problem with me seeing her. Jack wasn't around. They trusted me.

Getting closer to Sara was my true intention of being there. Everything else was a lie. Leaving town was the best thing for everyone. Sticking around and hitting on Sara reminded me how pathetic I was.

The longer I stayed here, the less likely I was to keep my secrets. When Sara and the others learned of my lies, my ass was grass. Using the name John was an example of my weak character. Such a person was not worthy of Sara's trust.

An untrustworthy person was a suspect for any case. Being a suspect exposed me to questions I wanted to avoid, such as why I didn't call for help or what I was doing in the Smoky Mountains.

I decided to come clean. Telling Sara the truth and suffering the consequences was my best path forward. What's the worst that could happen? Locking me in the psych unit was a joke. After what I'd been through, this place was a walk in the park. Even receiving a lobotomy was more welcome than keeping all my memories since leaving Southern California.

I turned to Sara, grabbed her by the shoulders, and said, "I have something I need to tell you."

She said, "Sure, what?"

Just as I was about to spill the beans, the door burst open, and Hammer Man came spilling into the room. His body odor dominated the air around us. It filled my nostrils with his sweat and the garlic from his last meal.

I said, "Oh my God, what is that smell?"

He said, "Who the hell are you?"

I said, "My name's John. Pleased to meet you."

I turned towards him and stuck my hand out. Jack looked at my hand and then looked me in the eyes. He said, "That's not going to happen."

Sara said, "This is Jack."

Jack and I faced off against each other, sizing one another up.

Sara said, "What were you going to tell me, John?"

I said, "Oh, I forgot."

Pointing out the stench of a large ape as he entered the room was not my best decision. The smell had shocked me. It had forced me to react even though I didn't want to. It was bad.

Jack said, "So, how do you know my sister?"

I pointed to Sara, "This one?"

He said, "No dimwit. The one you brought here."

Jack and I were not getting along. He acted like I was a lying sack of crap. He knew me better than I knew myself.

I said, "She hired me. I brought her here because I didn't know where else to go."

He said, "That's right. You were being helpful."

I admit, punching him in the face was something I really wanted to do. Reaching his fat head with my hands was another matter. He was tall and strong. If I attacked him, the most likely outcome involved him grabbing me by my head and throwing me to the ground.

I said, "Yes, I was."

He glowered. Somewhere in that thick, meaty head of his, I'd touched a nerve.

The tension between Jack and I filled the room. Everyone was quiet. The ladies seemed worried.

Sara said, "Jack, I need to talk with you. John, can you wait outside?"

I went to the hall. Oh, well. Because of Jack, living with Sara the rest of my life looked less likely. Even if I decided to stick it out here with her, dealing with Jack seemed hard. I doubted Jack would let Sara and I live in peace.

Sara came out. She said, "Want to get a cup of coffee?"

I said, "Sure."

We walked to a cafe close to the building's entrance. I sat down at a table while Sara bought us two cups of coffee. I watched her as she smiled at me and bounced her way to the table with a cup in each hand.

I said, "Thank you."

She said, "Listen. I'm sorry about Jack. He's a little upset, that's all. I reminded him of how our sister behaved when our parents died. He understands now."

I said, "Yeah, I shouldn't have said what I did about the smell. But I was just reacting. I didn't know he smelled that bad."

She said, "It's okay. He doesn't shower for days. And he loves Italian food."

We both laughed.

I loved spending time with Sara. She was fun with a good head on her shoulders. She was also a good person and treated me with more respect than anyone had in my life. She deserved to know who I really was.

She said, "So, when are you planning on going back to Los Angeles?"

I said, "I booked a flight for Friday."

Another lie.

She said, "Maybe, I can look you up if I head out there sometime."

"That would be great. I'd love that."

Although I did feel this way, I knew it was impossible for us to meet again. Once I left here, I planned on disappearing like a wet fart in the rain.

We didn't talk for a while after that. We both sat there looking at each other and smiling. That moment was really nice. It restored my faith in life, humanity and love.

I said, "You want to go for a walk?"

We strolled through a park adjacent to the psychiatric ward. We sat down on a bench underneath some maples and looked at a family of ducks in the lake. She grabbed my hand and held it in hers.

On the other side of the lake, I saw Hammer Man standing next to a tree, staring at us. When I realized the figure standing there was him and not one of the trees, I nearly jumped off the bench.

I said, "Crap, that guy is scary. Is he always like that?"

Looking towards where my eyes pointed and seeing Jack, Sara said, "Yes, unfortunately. He's just uptight and worried about his sisters."

My relationship with Jack was headed in a bad direction. Pulling it out of its death spiral was impossible. Both of us had made up our minds about the other. The best way to make it last without killing each other was to keep our distance.

Getting out of town sooner rather than later was a good idea. Staying away from Dr. Joyce's family until I departed was mandatory. Breaking off my relationship with Sara produced a painful but necessary outcome.

I turned to Sara. "So, you want to sleep with me at your sister's place tonight?"

Chapter 23

CLAY JOYCE

T he next morning, we found ourselves waking up to the voice of Sara's brother, Clay, on the phone. Clay was a dipstick. He was annoying beyond words. Asking his brothers and sisters for money and creating a life full of lies and chaos, Clay checked all the boxes for an impending human disaster. Although saying we were similar was not wrong; I fought this comparison with all my soul. I had a conscience after all.

On this phone call, he pleaded with Sara to send him travel money to see Dr. Joyce. She rolled her eyes and agreed, sending the money with her phone once they'd hung up. She believed Clay was probably already in town.

Clay's drinking caused problems for his whole family. He blew through their lives like a tornado. Even though he'd put all of them through hell with his lying, stealing and binge drinking, he never understood why they disliked him for it. He was doing what he needed to do.

That's why I refused to compare myself to him. Unlike him, my problems were not of my own making. A supernatural force pursued me, but nothing chose Clay. Clay made his own choices. Doing nothing about his drinking was his decision. He picked booze over his family.

Sara loved Clay. She didn't share my view of him. She never talked bad about him and tried to help him. Her brothers and sisters didn't like the support she gave him. They thought she fed his addiction and made his problems worse.

As Sara and I sat on her sister's couch watching television, there was a knock on the door. When Sara answered it, I heard her say, "Oh hi, Clay!"

Since we'd talked to him less than two hours prior, Sara's assumption seemed correct. He was in town this whole time. What a liar.

She said, "John, come meet Clay."

Lifting myself from the couch with the least enthusiasm possible, I walked to the door and offered a limp hand. Clay grabbed it with both of his and pumped it up and down.

He said, "Glad to meet you!"

"Glad to meet you."

We all sat down and watched television together.

Clay was fragile. He was undernourished and looked beaten down. Getting in his face or yelling at him were not advisable. He might lose the will to live.

After several hours of watching television and ignoring Clay's awkwardness, I came to a stark realization. Did Sara take me in like Clay because she saw me as helpless? Was I another Clay to her?

Thinking about this for a while, I realized something worse. Clay was sleeping here tonight.

Oh God, within a few hours of opening the door to this bozo, my life of happiness with Sara was taking a left turn to hell. Clay was a bastard.

When Sara and I decided to sleep, Clay said he needed to get something from the store and went out. He came back with a six pack and a bottle of hard liquor.

I thought to myself, "This is going to work out great."

Sure enough, later that night, Sara and I woke to the sound of Clay crying. We heard him saying things like, "Why, why, why? Mommy, Daddy!"

What a winner this guy was. Neither Sara nor I wanted to get out of bed and talk to him, so we let him ramble all night.

Clay was a real joy killer. His presence in the next room kept Sara and I from cuddling even though the door was shut. The safest distance from Clay was in the next state over.

Clay was the first person I wished the bugs ate. If there ever was a time we needed the bugs, the time was now. A planet without Clay would be a better planet.

In the morning, Sara worked on getting Jack ready while I stayed in bed. I heard her urging him to wake up, Clay whining, and then the front door slamming.

Opening the bedroom door and peering out, I made sure they were gone before walking into the living room with my tighty-whities on. Fixing myself a bagel and some coffee, I parked my butt on the couch. No longer worrying about living in Dr. Joyce's apartment felt good.

Even though I woke up a few moments ago and drank some coffee, I fell asleep a second time when I laid down on the couch. While my sleep the night before had been free of dreams, my dreams on the couch were troubled.

First, I heard buzzing which softened until it sounded more like a hum. Next, I opened my eyes to see the Joyces staring down at me. Sara, Jack and Clay were there. In the background stood the psychiatrist. They looked glum. Not a happy face in the group. I tried speaking and getting up, but I was paralyzed.

When I awoke from my second slumber, I jumped off the couch to see if I was still paralyzed. Getting into the shower, I lathered myself good. The hot water soothed my body.

When I turned off the water and opened the curtain to step out, a foul smell reached my nostrils. Looking around the bathroom, I noticed the toilet wasn't flushed. I knew right away who'd left the load floating there. Clay was a moron.

Wanting Clay to vanish from the face of the earth was at the top of my wish list. Never hearing his name again was a close second. I didn't make a lot of wishes before, so I hoped God heard this one.

Unfortunately, making this prayer was a bad idea for God did answer it. As the saying goes, be careful what you wish for since you just might get it.

Chapter 24

THE PROCEDURE

The psychiatrist said she heard a humming sound when she was with Dr. Joyce. Determined to find out what it was, she'd checked Dr. Joyce's medical files for implants and requested her family approve a CAT scan.

During the CAT scan, she discovered a mass towards the front of the neurocranium above Dr. Joyce's right eye socket. She recommended a biopsy of this mass to the Joyce family.

Sara didn't know how to feel about it. She considered getting a second opinion. Although the procedure the psychiatrist recommended was mild, it was still invasive.

The rest of the family planned on arriving soon, so she postponed the decision until their arrival. Sara joked about using me as a tiebreaker if the decision ended in a stalemate.

When the family's sisters and brother arrived, we met at a diner. At first, everyone assumed I was Sara's boyfriend. The atmosphere turned awkward when word spread that I was under the employ of Dr. Joyce as well. I didn't like talking about my employment since it forced me to lie, and it made my relationship with Sara seem amoral.

Joe was the last brother I needed to meet. He said, "So did Sara introduce you to my sister. Or was it the other way around?"

I said, "Actually, I didn't meet Sara until Dr. Joyce became sick and I brought her to the psychiatric ward."

Joe looked at me with a screwed-up face, as if processing my words short circuited his brain. Since my relationship with Dr. Joyce was a mystery, starting a romantic relationship with her sister when she became ill seemed odd. My reluctance to talk about it made it worse.

I said, "I just worked with the Doctor."

With the exception of Sara, who smiled, the rest of the table looked at me with dubious expressions. I felt their scrutiny of me. I was a crook.

Finding out the truth about me also put Sara's ass on the line. She was innocent. Like me, she followed her heart. Unlike me, she told the truth in all things. Her naivety for jumping in the sack with a con man might prove unforgivable to her family.

I sat between Sara's two other sisters. Like all the Joyce women, their hair was thick and black. Although Jennifer and Judy were attractive, Sara glowed. Her smile illuminated her surroundings. Her presence made everything better, even our dinner.

When we'd finished eating, the Joyce family discussed the Doctor's procedure. Knowing my place, I stayed out of it. Most agreed that the endoscopy was a good idea. There was no need to use me as a tiebreaker after all.

The planned procedure was for an endoscope to enter her nose and approach the mass in her brain above her eyes. On reviewing this mass, the psychiatrist might take a sample. No one seemed concerned about the procedure being dangerous. They were happy the psychiatrist had found a physical problem with Doctor Joyce which they could address.

When we finished for the night, everyone gave each other hugs and kisses. As Sara and I carried a drunk Clay to the doors and a car outside, I caught a few glances from her family members. They knew what Sara and I planned once we returned to Dr. Joyce's apartment.

Although we hadn't planned anything too nasty, our plans did include a whole lot of intimacy. The only problem was Clay, but I hoped he stayed passed out.

Once we arrived home, we deposited Clay on the sofa and started our funny business. We were so hot and heavy we passed out and didn't wake until the morning. When we came out of our room, Clay was still sleeping on the couch with his clothes on. No one had tucked the dummy in.

Sara busied herself with calling the psychiatrist and then her brothers and sisters with the date and time of the procedure. The psychiatrist decided that sooner was better than later and set it up for the following day.

When we arrived at the hospital, a medical assistant led us into a viewing room with chairs. We all sat down and looked through a window. On the other side of the window, Dr. Joyce lay on a table with the psychiatrist at her side and a few other assistants to help with her work.

At first, everything appeared normal. The psychiatrist took a long cord and shoved it up Dr. Joyce's nose. She looked on a monitor and maneuvered the endoscope here and there. When she arrived at the site of the mass, she gasped.

Over the intercom, we heard her say something like, "That can't be."

We all looked at each other.

She said, "There's something free and moving around in her brain. I don't know what it is. I'm going to touch it, but I'm not going to take a sample yet. I want to see how it reacts before I do anything else."

I heard a scream first. It may have come from the psychiatrist. I don't know. It was followed by chairs tipping over and men yelling. In front of us, the Doctor's head burst open in a whirlwind of blood and pieces of flesh. In this fountain of gore, a group of black insects swarmed into the room. After fileting the Doctor's face open, they circled the psychiatrist and her assistants, blocking them from our view.

I sprang into action. I was experienced in matters involving horrific bug acts. I grabbed Sara and headed for the door. She hesitated for a moment, so I picked her up with one arm and opened the door with the other, running into the hall.

I didn't stop running or put Sara down until we'd made our way to the psych unit's entrance and outside. Sara fell to her knees, crying. I put my arm around her and touched her face.

I said, "I'm sorry."

As we knelt, the rest of her family came running outside. Jack and Joe walked up to me. Jack said, "What the hell happened in there?"

I said, "How would I know?"

He grabbed me by my shirt with both hands and lifted me off the ground. He was a big boy. Pulling me to his face, he said, "Listen, dickhead, you tell me what those goddamn things are or I'm going to wipe the street with you."

I said, "I really don't know. There were some big bugs in the Smokies, but nothing like that. You think I would be here if there was?"

He threw me to the ground and said, "Yeah, right. This is your only warning. I want you out of town and away from our family by tomorrow."

I said, "What are you going to do if I don't?"

He said, "You know what I am going to do."

The rest of Sara's family looked at me with anger and fear. Their blame was misplaced. I didn't control what the bugs did.

After standing up, I walked to Sara and helped her to her feet. While I was holding her, a staffer came out of the hospital.

He said, "We have control of the situation, and the authorities are on their way."

Joe said, "What happened to our sister?"

He said, "We are still assessing everything. Due to the nature of the incident, we have put the hospital under quarantine."

126

Joe didn't ask if Dr. Joyce was alive, but everyone knew the answer.

After hearing the word "quarantine," I wanted out of there. Serving a quarantine at the Doctor's apartment was much better than the psych unit.

I said, "Can we leave?"

Everyone looked at me with pained faces. Asking this question confirmed to them that I was a selfish puke.

He said, "I would wait until the authorities get here. When they say you can leave, you are free to do so."

When the police did arrive, they brought with them a hazmat response team. They performed physical check-ups and interviewed all of us. Lucky for me, they didn't ask me many questions about the Doctor. When they asked me about my involvement, I told them I was Sara's boyfriend.

Hazmat teams, cops and questions made me nervous. I carried the wallet of a dead man and assumed his identity. My lies were close to engulfing me. I imagined the look of disappointment on Sara's face when she found out.

The process took hours, but they let us go. Sara was exhausted. She cried the whole time we were there.

I said, "Let's go, baby."

Dr. Joyce's madness was over. My madness began.

Chapter 25

MADNESS

The first thing I did was rent a car. After putting a slipcover over it, I parked it behind Dr. Joyce's apartment. If I needed to bail, the car offered me a quick escape.

When I rented the car, I used John's identification and wore a hat. Our faces were similar enough for me to get by security.

Since that night, my relationship with Sara wasn't the same. Her trust in me suffered and she avoided intimacy with me. It was a drag.

She asked me, "Why did you say you were sorry?"

I said, "What are you talking about?"

She said, "After my sister's procedure, you said you were sorry. Why?"

I said, "I don't know. I felt bad. That's all."

She said, "It just seems odd that you would say that."

I said, "Why's it odd to try and comfort someone after what happened?"

She looked away. The damage was done. That night, our relationship ran face first into a hurdle of distrust, blowing our trust to smithereens.

With a car out back, my departure came into focus. I loved Sara but I didn't know if she loved me. Feeling grateful for a bad experience only works if it helps someone you love. I appreciated the bugs for forcing me to see how I hurt Sara. If I loved her, I would free her. I would leave.

A few days later, she left to see someone but didn't say who. She was not the same as before. Our love was on the skids and rattling down the drain. By hiding her plans, she'd hinted to me that I should leave her. Did I want to wait until she actually told me to leave? Forcing her to tell me was not an act of love.

I sat down in a chair next to the couch where Clay lay with a bottle in his hand. He said, "You know, no one likes you."

Great, now Captain Dumbass was taking cheap shots at me.

I said, "So?"

He said, "So, you should leave."

I said, "Or what? Are you going to make me leave, Bottle Boy?"

He said, "You know you shouldn't make fun of people's problems."

I said, "The only problem here is your mouth. So shut your hole."

Suddenly, the buzzing overcame me. This time it was stronger. Unable to see, I heard a loud bang and blacked out.

When I awoke, I lay at the foot of the chair. Clay was gone. I stood up, searched the apartment and looked out the front door, but there was no sign of him. He was gone like a fart in the wind.

Wondering if I'd imagined what happened or if Clay really existed was just wishful thinking. I decided that Clay went out for a bottle while I passed out.

I fixed myself a sandwich and sat down on the couch. The apartment was nice with no one around. Taking a break from people provided an unexpected relief. Seeing Sara as the most stressful thing in my life surprised me. The bastard Clay was right. The time for packing my bags, throwing them in the trunk and burning rubber was now.

No one came home that night. Those jerks. They wanted me to leave. Like leaving the window open for a fly to flutter out, Clay and Sara stayed away hoping for me to leave. I refused to give them the satisfaction. If she wanted me to leave, Sara had to tell me.

Sitting in the chair, I stayed up as long as possible before going to bed. After nodding off with my head on my chest, I awoke in the morning with Sara kicking my feet.

She said, "Where the hell is Clay?"

I said, "I thought he was with you?"

She said, "Don't be funny. Where is he?"

I said, "I'm not. I don't know where he went. Maybe he went to get a bottle and found a party."

She said, "I thought you were leaving. That you scheduled a flight?"

I said, "Don't worry, I'll be out of your hair soon enough. Where were you last night?"

"I stayed with Jack."

I said, "Honey, you know he doesn't like me."

She said, "Yeah, but you being here complicates everything."

"Sara, I didn't choose all of this. I only want to be with you."

"I know."

She sat down on the bed, and we hugged each other. Testing relationships makes them stronger. Sara's warm embrace reminded me of our love for each other and its promise of a future together.

We turned off our phones for the day and sat together on the couch. We didn't watch any television or talk very much. We let the quiet comfort us. Clay's absence helped.

That night, we slept together holding each other. Our sleep was warm and restful. How pleasant life is when people get along.

The next morning, when we turned on our phones, Sara's email and voicemail were filled with messages from her brothers and sisters who'd been trying to reach her. On checking them, we discovered Clay was dead.

We were shocked. Some hikers found his body a few miles from Dr. Joyce's apartment in the woods. There were no access roads or hiking trails near the site. As a matter of fact, there were no footprints or signs of a struggle at all. On the news, they said several of his bones were broken and he died from internal bleeding.

When the police came to interview us, I told them that he'd left to buy some booze and that was the last time I saw him. I didn't say anything about blacking out and waking up to find him gone.

When they left, Sara asked me, "What do you remember?"

I said, "Just him leaving."

She said, "That's it? He didn't say anything about where he was going?"

I said, "No, he was his regular self. I thought he was going out to buy some booze."

All of this was tough on Sara. She stopped crying because she'd ran out of tears. She was haggard. Within a few days, her whole world turned upside down. A woman living her whole life believing love and empathy conquered all now found herself surrounded by darkness.

At that point, we were in trouble, but we didn't know the source of the menace. Did the bugs get him? Did he piss off the liquor store clerk?

A grim idea stuck itself to the back of my mind. If someone killed him, could that someone be me? I wanted him gone but not "gone." Did I black out and kill him with a split personality? I didn't feel like I had a second personality. Did the bugs infest me and make me kill him? There were no holes in my skin, and I didn't feel sick.

Sara suspected me. Sometimes, out of the corner of my eye, I caught her looking at me. She started asking me questions, like "Did you and Clay fight?" or "Did he say anything to upset you?"

How we treated each other changed. When we watched the news, we sat on opposite ends of the couch and didn't talk much. When we went to bed, we both stayed on our sides. She didn't trust me, and I didn't trust myself either.

The next day, when I woke up, she whispered to someone on her phone. I assumed it was Jack. When she heard me, she hung up.

She said, "I might go somewhere tonight."

I said, "That's fine. I need to get my stuff packed."

She said, "Are you leaving?"

I said, "Yeah, I'd better. We talked about this before."

"We did. But why now?"

I said, "This place is getting weird."

"It sure is."

While she told me this, Sara was not her normal kind self. She looked stern. All of this death overwhelmed her. It was too much for me too.

As we sat on opposite ends of the couch, the buzzing hit me again and blacked me out. When I came to, Sara was gone. I searched the apartment. When I didn't find her, I looked throughout the building and the surrounding parking lot. Still not finding her, I jumped in my car and drove in a circle around the complex for miles without success.

Did something take her? Did I do something to her? Did she just leave?

The evil surrounding me hijacked my thoughts. It told me I wasn't safe, not even in my own skin. It promised destruction of my soul and everything around me.

Sleeping and eating weren't possible. Thinking straight was difficult. I watched television without knowing what I watched.

Later that night, there was a knock on my door. Looking through the peephole, I saw Jack. He was the last person I wanted to see.

I opened the door and said, "Hey."

He hit me with a right cross which almost took my head off. Falling onto my back a good four feet from the door and hitting my head on the floor, my body was in no condition to defend itself as Jack stood over me and started kicking me.

One kick took the breath out of me. Another one bent my ribs. The last one landed right on my balls. Jack was a cruel son of a bitch.

He said, "You are not going to hurt my family anymore! My parents almost killed all of us! You are not going to do the same thing. You hear me? I know you aren't John O'Neill. I looked you up. Sara sent me a picture of your license."

I stammered, "What are you talking about?"

He said, "You killed Sara. You dropped her in the middle of the street, just like Clay. You sick son of a bitch."

I said, "No, I didn't. I have been here the whole time."

He said, "Enough of your lying crap. It's game over for you."

He walked to the kitchen, opened one of the drawers and pulled out a hammer. He smiled and swung the hammer once or twice to feel its weight.

He said, "Party time."

I pushed myself up. Getting to my legs was a matter of survival. Deep down I somehow found the strength, but no sooner did I stand up then the buzzing hit me again. Of all the times it needed to make its presence known!

When I came to, Hammer Man was no longer there. The whole apartment was quiet with the door still open. Everything was surreal, causing me to question my own sanity. The pain from Jack's kicks and punches brought me back down to earth. The good news was the bastard was gone.

After closing the door, I went to the kitchen, grabbed a knife and held my arm over the sink. There was no more running for me. Of all the death and destruction, I was the common denominator. Time to do the world a favor and end it. Time to finish what Jack started.

When I was about to carve my wrist, the sudden realization that Jack was a dumbass hit me. Of course he wanted me dead. Hammer Man was an idiot. I wasn't so dumb. There was a reason for all of this. Not giving up is what I needed to do. I put the knife in the back of my pants just in case.

After packing my bags and throwing the keys on the kitchen counter, I gave the apartment one final look. Here, there'd been moments of peace and happiness. There were also moments of doubts, betrayal, and death. Within the four walls of Dr. Joyce's apartment, I'd lived a full life in less than a month.

I took the elevator down to the lobby and walked out to my car. Pulling the tarp off of it and putting my luggage in the trunk, my plan was to get behind the wheel and haul ass, but it didn't work out.

Driving down the road, I heard someone yelling. At first, it was distant, then the yelling came closer and closer, until it was on top of me. I looked through the car windows. Front, side and back, I saw nothing, until I turned back to the front and a large mass landed with a thud in front of my car.

After opening the door and stepping out, I peered over the hood of the car and saw a body lying there. It looked a lot like Jack.

I said, "Poor, dumb, hammer-loving bastard."

Behind me, someone said, "He sure was."

Turning around, I saw the psychiatrist standing a few feet behind me. She was wearing a muumuu.

I said, "Why are you wearing a muumuu?"

She said, "Where are you going? "

I said, "The hell away from here."

She said, "Why?"

I said, "Um, bodies falling from the sky. And I almost wiped out an entire family."

She said, "She wants you to join us. She wants you to know peace from all of this. All you have to do is believe."

I said, "No thanks. My plan is to travel back to California and get a fast-food job."

She said, "You know that's not practical. And this isn't going to end. This is just the beginning."

I said, "Well, if your beginning involves killing everything in sight, it's not going to last very long."

She said, "It's not for everyone. Here, let me show you something."

She lifted her head to the sky and spread her arms. From her back sprang long spider legs. The coxa hung there for a brief moment, until chitin rolled from them and sprouted black wings.

As I mouthed the words, "What in the hell," she grabbed me around the waist with her tarsus' and shot straight up into the air.

Our ascension was so fast, I almost passed out from the g-forces. Once above the clouds, she folded her wings and dove back down. After going back through the clouds, she spread out her wings again and glided in circles.

She said, "Look at how humans dirty this beautiful earth with their garbage, like a virus."

I didn't say anything. I was dizzy and cold as hell.

I looked at her body. Small black bugs moved all around it devouring its flesh and replacing it with larvae. The bugs' transformation of her seemed painful.

She said, "I know it's a lot to take in. But we want what's best for you. Don't you want to live free from worry? Free from the stress of life?"

I said, "You killed Sara."

She said, "Yes."

At this, I reached around and pulled out the knife in the back of my pants. Swinging my arm in an arc, I brought the knife down on her head.

When the knife penetrated her skull, it made a sound like the crushing of a bug. In response to a knife piercing her insect brain, her eyes crossed, and the downward spiral of her flight made tighter and tighter circles until our trajectory went straight down.

I yelled, "Yah, Bitch!"

Positioning her under me, we hit the ground hard with a splat. A cloud of bugs flew up and away. I rolled off her body. Covered in bug juice, I touched my body all over to make sure I wasn't damaged.

136

Jumping to my feet, I headed in the direction of where I thought my car might be. Killing the psychiatrist was satisfying. I ended the one who brought me so much pain. Her death was the end of at least one sucky chapter of my life.

When I arrived back at my car, no one was around. The time was late. I'm sure no one wanted to stop for what looked like a crime scene.

Looking down at Hammer Man's body, I noticed the insect bitch had broken his arms and tied them behind his back. His last hours with her were rough indeed.

Slipping behind the wheel, I put on my seat belt and hit the accelerator. In case someone did call the authorities about a dead body in the road, leaving as fast as possible would be a good idea.

Not looking in the rear view, I knew one thing. It was time to go home.

Chapter 26

CALIFORNIA HERE I COME

U sing the old Route 66 was the best route to California. Its access point was close to my current location and its corridor was a straight line to the west.

Route 66 is historic. Its promotion lured people to sunny California. Real estate firms exploited the California sunshine, drawing people from dark places like New York. Lord knows I was sick of the darkness – and the bugs.

Staying overnight in superstore parking lots was great. They offered free parking with no questions asked, and leaving as soon as the sun rose didn't draw suspicion.

Although traveling both day and night was possible, I avoided the nighttime since I needed rest and, for whatever reason, my bug experiences were bad. I credited this to the awful summoning I'd witnessed in New Mexico and the Smoky Mountains.

Bugs occupied bodies day and night. Such a fact invited speculation that they needed cover from the sun. I didn't think so. They weren't afraid of sunlight. They were afraid of being found out.

Those goddamn bugs were getting stronger. The day their antennae popped out in the cold light of day was the first day of the apocalypse.

Driving in my car, the thought of veering off the main highway and becoming lost in the Midwest did cross my mind. The diversion would be the best chance of escape from the authorities and the bugs, but I drove on. Meeting my end soon was a foregone conclusion. By hesitating to kill me, the bugs had given me the discretion of choosing the place.

Why the bugs waited to kill me or take me over, I found puzzling. Everyone else was dead, but not me. John and I followed the same path to the bugs. They also hesitated in his infestation. They blew him up in the cave, but he'd had a chance to flee like me.

The reason for sparing me lay in the image – and my belief in the image. Joy was not a believer – but John and I were. We became that way once we saw what happened to Joy.

Seeing myself as the first real follower of "She Who Shall Not Be Named," in the modern era was not far-fetched. Her bugs infested people without belief. Receiving salvation from my belief in her was plausible.

This was a lot of speculation on my behalf. After all, knowing what the rotters and everyone else went through was not possible, but by now, I considered myself an end of the world expert.

Understanding why "She Who Shall Not Be Named" needed belief or followers was another matter. She wanted to give us more than a god. She wanted to give us a choice.

She was one sick bastard. Offering a person the choice of being consumed by bugs or dropping them to their death from the sky was not a choice I liked to make. Her religion was a death cult.

Dry bug juice covered my clothes. My smell was a cross between sour milk and flat beer. I credited this to the remains of my cologne and not having showered for days. When I arrived back at the fraternity, I doubted my brothers would even notice.

I was serious about fast food. The minimum wage offered by such a position didn't pay my student loans, but I didn't care. I wanted a job with as little responsibility as possible.

With the end of the world crawling up my ass, free fast food and some extra cash sounded real good.

Chapter 27

FAST FOOD

Fast food was a mistake. Every night, I smelled like tacos. I crashed hard but hated the idea of going to work when I woke up.

My brothers didn't say anything about it, although I guessed they didn't like my smell. As far as they knew, I enrolled in the fall semester. Living at the house required me to be a full-time student, but my enrollment status was not required until the end of summer. I foresaw the end of the world happening well before then.

For the first time in the history of our house, I was the smart one. Those idiots were ignorant of the hell that awaited them. A hell brewing in the darkest holes on earth, waiting to come forth and devour human flesh.

Sitting on a stool at our house bar, I imagined the looks of confusion and horror on their faces as the bugs blew out our windows and flew down the throats of my brothers. After turning them into empty hulks or blowing them apart like giant flesh balloons, the bugs would face me. What would they do? Fly past me onto their next house party? Or was my time finally up?

Some of my brothers asked me about John and Joy. I told them that they'd decided to camp in the Smoky Mountains until the end of summer.

Living out the rest of my days with full drama was not appealing. Telling my house fratters, alerting the authorities or even appearing on the news were great ways to get everyone's attention, but I liked the idea of spending my last two months in peace.

141

The only hiccup came when John's father called the house. He wanted to know why his son wasn't calling him. I responded that John's campsite was out of cell range.

My fast-food job became easier. Once I'd learned everything in my current position, I started performing different roles. I cooked, prepared orders and rang out customers. I liked getting good at my job. It made me feel better than worthless.

One of the people I worked with was Suzie. I talked to her about everything. I don't know if she understood me or thought I was joking. She just nodded and said, 'Oh wow.'

Trusting people who worked in fast food came easy. No one talked about their jobs outside of work. And we had rough backgrounds. When I shared my stories with someone like Suzie, they probably thought my crazy stories were part of some trauma suffered as a child or adolescent.

One time, I told her about John. How he really wanted to get the image we saw and how his leg exploded out of that hole with his shoe still on it and she said, "Ay caramba."

At our restaurant, televisions hung in the lobby where people ordered food. Our customers watched them while they waited. One day, a news story came from Antarctica, which showed huge sand pits at the edge of a retreating glacier. The news was incredible since sand didn't exist in Antarctica before then.

No one thought that much about it. The customers were nonplussed and the workers even more so. I freaked out.

I ran around screaming that the world was ending. I tore off my hat and shirt. I cried and pulled my hair. My manager came out and slapped me. It froze me. While standing there, Suzie came up, took me by my hand, led me outside, and sparked a joint with me. When we mellowed out and went back inside an hour later, the manager gave me

142

a formal write-up and told me not to do it again. I was a good worker, and she didn't want to lose me. She gave me the rest of the day off.

Convincing people of the end of the world was hard. People were numb to hearing the world was ending. You might as well persuade someone they won the lotto.

The weekend after my work meltdown, Suzie invited me to a family gathering. She said, "gathering," but what she meant was an adult drinking party where the kids played in a separate room.

I was happy to go. I was desperate for a distraction. A head full of evil was like living in a bad neighborhood. With so many threats, I didn't know what to worry about first. The bugs eating the world, my fratters committing me to an asylum, or getting fired from my taco job, all carried equal weight in my mind.

At the party, Suzie hung with her sisters and left me to fend for myself. I ended up on the couch with that one odd cousin who didn't like talking with his own family but was okay with strangers.

His name was Ricky. He was a big believer in UFOs, so we hit it off pretty well.

He said, "Imagine if aliens lived here since the dawn of time. And all our deities and stuff were aliens with superpowers."

I said, "That's pretty far out. But imagine if they lived here this whole time deep in the earth, waiting to be awakened."

He said, "You mean, like maybe it was some bug alien race. And they hibernated here. And they could only arise if they found a true believer or worshipper to awaken them."

I said, "Yes, exactly."

He said, "No, that's too crazy."

Even among like-minded individuals, finding believers in the end of the world was impossible.

Suzie sat down next to me on the couch. "So, I see you've met Eddy."

I said, "Yeah."

She said, "I knew you two would hit it off well. You had a tough week, yeah?"

I said, "Yes, thanks for the doobie. That helped."

"No problem. I know how hard fast food can get sometimes."

Ricky said, "I also work in fast food."

Suzie said, "Don't you sell chicken?"

He said, "Yeah, it's all I eat."

I said, "I love tacos."

They both stopped and looked at me. Seeing all my friends consumed by bugs had made me awkward in social settings.

Suzie said, "I'm going to get some chips. Be right back."

Ricky said, "Me too."

And, just like that, I was alone. Spending time with other people helped. At the frat, we hung around each other during parties but that was about it. Getting out and meeting new people did my heart good. My outlook on life was less dire.

When I returned to the frat house that night, one of my brothers told me that John's dad called again. That call was his fifth call in two weeks. His concern for his son was serious.

Telling John's parents the truth was not practical. They deserved the truth but a believable one. My truth was so fantastic, I didn't believe it myself. Giving them a perceived fictional account of what happened risked traumatizing them more.

I believed the world was ending with all my soul. After what I'd experienced, there was no denying the horrible fate which awaited the world and all its inhabitants.

For my last days, eating tacos and spending time with other people was all I wanted. Too bad for me that John's parents had other ideas.

Chapter 28

PRIVATE DICK

Not believing my story, John's father hired a private investigator from Los Angeles. Before the investigator introduced himself to me, I caught him following me. It was easy. Wearing a fake mustache and wig, he stood out like a sore thumb. By making dramatic turns with his head when I looked at him, he betrayed his interest in me.

Judging by the guy's lack of professionalism, he was on the low end of private dicks. Even if his wages were one step above fast food, he was still a bigger loser than me; at least my food was free. John's father was one cheap guy.

My curiosity getting the better of me, I waited behind a building for him, to find out why he followed me. When he came walking around the corner, I jumped in front of him.

I said, "Who are you?"

He said, "Who me?"

"Yeah you. And why are you wearing that stupid mustache and wig?"

He blushed. "You have a friend named John?"

I said, "Yes."

He said, "His father thinks he's missing, and that you know why."

I said, "Why are you following me though?"

"Well, John's father said you are avoiding talking to him."

I said, "I'm not. I just don't know where he is exactly."

"As far as we know, you were the last person to see him."

I said, "Listen, why don't you come by the house sometime and I will tell you everything I know?"

He stared at me and said, "Sure."

When we parted ways, he watched me as I walked away. He didn't like me. He sensed I was a rat. He was right.

By hiring the private dick, John's father upended my plans for my last few months of life on planet earth. My inability to control him or his private dick aggravated me. They were a problem, but ignorant of the actual bucket of crap about to drop on all of us. I planned on playing along with their idiot investigation.

When we met, the first thing the dick asked me was, "You say Joy traveled with you and John to the Smokies?"

I said, "Yes, that's right."

He said, "If that's the case, then why didn't she fly there with you and John?"

"Pardon?"

He said, "I only found flight itineraries for you and John. How did she get to the Smokies?"

This was bad.

I said, "How do I know? I don't know anything about all that."

He said, "They found a car John rented not far from here. It was burned inside and out but the car company still identified it. You know anything about that?"

This was a worse situation than I planned for. He knew me better than I knew myself. He had my ass in a sling. To get out of this required some serious lying.

I said, "Wow, that's crazy. Any suspects?"

He said, "Yeah, you."

So much for my lying.

I said, "Why exactly is that?"

He said, "Simple. There's no one else."

I said, "Okay, how about I show you where he was last?"

"How?"

I said, "On a map."

He said, "I have a better idea, why don't you take me there."

I said, "What?"

He said, "Why don't we travel to the Smokies so you can show me where you last saw John?"

This idiot didn't know that his request was a death wish. Lord only knew what hell waited for us there.

Since the Smokies were on the opposite end of the country in the middle of nowhere, traveling there was painful and impractical for him as well. I took a chance and called his bluff.

I said, "Sure."

"Great, let's leave this coming Monday. I can buy the tickets and hotel."

This guy was a moron. Besides New York, the Smokies were the last place on planet earth I wanted to visit again. I planned on missing the flight.

I said, "Sounds good."

"Great. I will come here to pick you up. Also, just to make you aware, I found an itinerary of John traveling to New York, but I didn't find one for you. He used his credit card to pay for the flight. You know, using a stolen credit card to travel across state lines is a federal crime."

What a bastard. He knew I was a criminal. Fine. Even if he wanted to die, I refused to die with him. At the first sign of trouble, he was on his own.

I said, "I understand."

Waiting for our plane to take-off to Asheville reminded me of my travels with John and Joy. Back then, the excitement of our journey filled me with hope. Now, the memories of my friends filled me with dread.

No matter how hard I tried to avoid them, the bugs kept calling for me. They played with me, by killing everyone I loved and forcing me to watch.

As I looked at the dick sitting next to me with his head in a magazine, bitter feelings came alive in me. Such an ignorant, selfish ass deserved whatever the bugs planned on giving him. By convincing himself that I was the answer to all his problems, he wanted me to relive the loss and pain of my friends dying.

He didn't want any answers from me. My answers promised pain and death for everyone. He wasn't safe. No one was.

I hated the idea of flying back to the Smokies and the evil that waited for me there. I belonged in fast food and not in a bug pit in North Carolina. This sad little man was the reason for my reversal of fortune.

I said, "I hope you like bugs."

With his headphones on, he didn't hear me but caught my lips moving. He took his headphones off and said, "What did you say?"

I said, "What do you want?"

He looked into my eyes. Seeing the scorn and disdain in them, he turned away and put his headphones back on.

For the remainder of the flight, I looked straight ahead. Traumatized people stare off into space for hours, unaware of the passage of time. Remembering my last trip to the Smokies while our plane bounced along the clouds put me in a similar state.

When the wheels of our plane touched down, my mind was distant and tired. I didn't remember anything about our flight, even though I was awake the whole time.

I said, "Is the trip over yet?"

He heard me this time and said, "You wish."

For once the dummy was right. I wished for the trip to end. Unlike him, I avoided places of death.

Renting a car instead of an SUV gave me a sense of relief. Looking at an SUV plagued me with memories of my travels with

Joy and John. A car was also easier for me to drive in case I returned to the airport alone.

As we traveled the same highway as before, a memory of John made its way to the front of my mind. I remembered the long silence of our last ride together. A wall existed between us. John's determination and anger had created this wall. His search for the image and Joy's death turned him suicidal. He was hell-bound.

Some might say I was hell-bound on a similar path as John. My driver and I didn't like each other. He wanted me in jail. I wanted him gone. Like John and I, we shared a wall of anger. But, as the saying goes, "Tear down one wall…. fall into a bug pit."

Chapter 29

RETURN TO SMOKY MOUNTAIN

We turned off the highway down the gravel road leading to the park's parking lot. The ranger was nowhere in sight. Coming here was as grim as the last time.

We parked our car a few spots from where John parked the SUV and walked to the tree line. The private investigator knew this was a camping expedition and had packed tents and food. The Smokies were huge. Traveling in them took days or weeks.

I gave the dick a compass location in the opposite direction of the Mud Caves. I did not want him finding John's leg or encountering the bug people.

Our first day was uneventful and quiet. He tried to make conversation with me, but I ignored him. Sleeping that night was peaceful.

By twilight of the second day, we were close to the compass location. The investigator grew excited, and I grew worried. My stomach churned and my skin prickled.

He said, "When we get there tomorrow, try to remember exactly where he camped."

"I will."

He said, "Hopefully he's still there."

"Hopefully."

There was no hope for me or of finding John. When he saw an empty campsite, or remains of one, my ruse was over. I pictured the dick putting leg irons on me for my walk back to the car.

I didn't sleep. This was it. Tomorrow was the beginning of the end for me.

The private investigator woke early. He stuck his head in my tent and yelled for me to get up. He wanted to get to John's non-existent campsite as soon as possible.

As he bounded through the forest like a jackass, I trudged behind. My goal was to slow him down but preventing an idiot from running through a forest is hard. Whenever he found himself too far ahead of me, he stopped and yelled, "Don't worry, I'll wait for you to catch up!"

Sneaking off in the opposite direction did cross my mind. Going anywhere else in the Smoky mountains was a pleasant idea, but there were too many unknowns. Fear kept me from leaving. Bugs eating me, getting lost and starving to death, or escaping back to Los Angeles only to find the cops waiting at my door all conspired to dampen any bravery which remained in me.

When we arrived at John's mythical location, he said, "We're here."

His earlier excitement turned to concern and disappointment. He said, "No one's here."

He looked around and said, "Doesn't look like anyone's been here in a while."

I thought, *they were never here, you jackass.*

After staying quiet for a while, he said, "Are you telling me everything you know?"

I said, "Of course! You think I like coming here, only to spend a lot of days walking around for no reason?"

He took out his binoculars and walked up the hill we stood on. Scanning the horizon from whence we'd came, he said, "What's that?"

I said, "What's what?"

He handed me the binoculars and I looked through them. Holy crap, there was something shining off in the distance in the direction of the Mud Caves. HIs finding John's leg and shoe were enough to put me in the slammer forever.

He said, "Let's go that way." "Sounds good."

I'd dodged a bullet for now. He didn't suspect me of lying yet, but if he found John's remains, he might suspect me of a whole lot more.

The day or two of travel time to our next destination gave me time to think of my next course of action. In the event we discovered John's bones, I roleplayed in my mind how to act surprised; and if we didn't, how to act disappointed.

As we walked towards the Mud Caves, the absurdity of the situation forced itself on me. Hoping to avoid being caught in a lie, I followed an investigator to the scene of the crime. Hoping to avoid persecution for my crimes of lunacy, I walked headfirst into death.

That night, when we put out our tents and lay down our bed rolls, I was at peace. Somehow, I knew everything was okay. A dream came to me.

"She Who Shall Not Be Named" was gigantic. On the snow and sand she towered miles above me. As she unfolded her dark wings, they blacked out the entire night sky.

She said, "Don't worry little one. Although this world will be consumed and destroyed, I have chosen you to live in peace. Believe in me and your woes of this god-forsaken planet will be swept away."

As she said the last part, she shook her huge wings and a horde of insects miles wide flew out of them. The wind of their flight knocked me to the ground. Whatever their destination, the swarm promised annihilation.

When I awoke, the private investigator stood outside my tent, waiting for me. He said, "Is there something you want to tell me?"

"No."

He said, "This morning, I woke early and hiked to the location we spied yesterday. You and I should both go there so you can see what I'm talking about."

This day started bad and became worse. We both knew what he'd found.

After getting dressed and packing, I followed him like a convict on his way to the gallows. Of all the different options rolling in my mind, bolting from him appeared the best. Some patience and a good distraction were all I needed.

As I watched him with my head hung low, I bided my time. This guy sucked. He deserved whatever came for him. I wasn't going to wait around and share his fate.

I recalled my dream and the peace it promised. Although for some reason I believed its message of peace, obtaining it was a different matter. "She Who Shall Not Be Named" forgot to provide the instructions.

That's the problem when an evil god from another dimension calls on you; they never tell you what they want.

Chapter 30

FREEDOM FORCE

A s we made our way to the clearing where John's leg spent its last days, the dick walked ahead of me. After walking to the river, he said, "Well, can you explain this?"

I looked over the area. Next to the river, there were several sand pits. Except in spaces occupied by boulders from the explosion, they were everywhere.

I said, "I don't know."

He said, "Well, if I traveled here, I think I would make note of large sand pits that people could fall into."

I said, "These weren't here before."

He said, "Sure. You don't think we are going to find John at the bottom of one of these?"

Surveying the clearing once more, I saw John's boney leg next to one of the pits. His shoe was still on it. I guess bugs don't like shoes. I said, "No, not at the bottom."

The investigator followed my gaze. When his eyes landed on the leg, he yelled, "Holy crap!"

Walking over to it, he said, "That's your ass, son. It's over for you now."

He pulled out a gun. Turning it in my direction, he said, "Sit down and put your hands behind you so I can cuff you."

I sat down on a stump with my arms behind me and my head down. At least he came prepared with a gun and cuffs.

As I heard his footsteps approaching me, I considered bolting, but the treeline was too far. Plugging me with a few rounds from a .357 was child's play. The leading candidate for a coup de grace was a bullet up my sphincter.

While waiting for the cold irons to touch my arms, I heard a loud scream. Looking up, I saw large silver bugs consuming the dick. They were the size of large dogs. The reflection of the sun on the carapaces blinded me. Their beacons shone like lighthouses.

With the bugs biting his arms and legs, he yelled, "Get my gun and get them off me!"

On the ground, a severed hand held the gun. It was a few feet from one of the bugs.

I backed away and said, "Sorry, man."

His face contorted in a mixture of confusion and anger. When he was about to speak again, one of the bugs crawled over the top of him and bit his head clean off. As his body fell to the ground, blood gushed from the stump of his neck.

I shouted, "Holy crap!" As I turned to run, I saw a bundle of dynamite fly over my head in the direction of the bug pits. It landed next to the investigator's geyser, rolling to a stop and revealing a short fuse.

I was in stride when the blast hit me. I flew from the riverbed all the way to the forest. My head missed a tree trunk by a few inches.

Stunned by the blast, I lay there helpless. Burns covered my right arm. My teeth protruded from my right cheek. Blood poured down my chin and chest.

All that remained of the investigator, insects, boulders, and sand were rocks and sticks. Whoever threw the dynamite blew the bugs and private dick straight to hell.

A bearded man with a trucker hat stood over me. He was an upgraded version of the Doofers. He yelled at me,, but I didn't hear him. I was deaf from the blast. I didn't say anything since my jaw was pinned by my teeth in my cheek. I was a mess.

As he walked away, I staggered to my feet and followed him. Unable to walk in a straight line, I grabbed his arm. He didn't pull away, allowing me to lean on him as we walked.

A few other men accompanied us. They walked on our right and left, keeping watch.

After the sunset, we made camp less than a mile from the clearing. Thankfully, my tent and sleeping bag had not been blown to hell.

When I sat down, one of the men walked over to me and grabbed my face. In one yank, he pulled my teeth out of my cheek. Once I finished screaming, he handed me a small towel drenched in whiskey. Putting it in my mouth, I applied pressure to stop the bleeding.

With the towel wrapped around my face, I started making my tent. By the time I laid down on my sleeping bag, my hearing came back. Before falling asleep, I walked over to the first man I'd met. He was by a fire in the middle of camp.

Through my mouth bandage, I said, "Thank you for saving me back there."

He said nothing. He busied himself with the fire, so I let him finish.

Off in the distance, I saw the steeple of the church outlined in the twilight. Sam's body remained there, making the spire look like a lollipop.

He said, "Why are you out here? Who was that being eaten by the bugs?"

I said, "That guy was a private investigator. He forced me to come out here."

He said, "Why did he force you?"

I said, "I came out here camping with a friend of mine. He disappeared. The investigator thought I could help find him."

He said, "I have also been looking for someone."

I said, "Who's that?"

He said, "My cousin, Sam."

The steeple of the church poked above the treeline. I didn't say a word.

He put his hand out. He said, "My name is Ronco Duffer."

For some reason, I had a habit of meeting losers. I said, "My pleasure."

He said, "You are welcome to leave us. But in your state, I suggest staying. We're going to see my brother tomorrow."

I said, "Your brother?"

He said, "Yeah, Bronco."

Oh great.

I said, "Where are you meeting him?"

He said, "Above us are some buildings. We believe this is the last place Sam went."

He had no idea how right he was. Even now, Sam liked hanging around there...

I said, "Sounds good."

The thought of seeing the bugs again hurt my brain. A bug reunion was a bad idea for a party. A vision of our bodies stacked on top of Sam's flashed across my mind.

We were close to the bugs. Staying here or going to the buildings would make little difference when it came to avoiding them. Since I lacked the strength for escape, staying with my group was my best chance for survival. Once I was fit, I vowed to get the hell out of there.

After putting my head down for the night, my mind went through my day. I laughed. Since he'd exploded, the private investigator hadn't entered my thoughts. I didn't miss him at all. Imagine living a life of such little consequence.

Dying here was an unhappy ending for anyone. Your mourners were insects. Even so, my end promised to pay my debts. It whispered absolution for my lies and the deaths of my loved ones.

That night, my sleep was uneventful. No dreams. Nothing. Maybe my newfound goddess abandoned me. I doubted I was so lucky.

All the men woke early. We didn't exchange pleasantries. We ate our breakfast bars in silence.

I rolled up my bed and tent like a drunk soldier. The trauma of the blast from the day before blurred my senses. Moving my body around challenged and worried me. When the time came to run, strong legs were important. The bugs liked nothing better than chasing after some idiot with spaghetti legs.

I followed the Duffers as we walked up a hill towards lumber town. They didn't talk much. Like the Doofers, they spoke with their fists and assault rifles.

Silly hillbillies. Conventional weapons were useless against the bugs. Hauling ass was a better strategy. Although guns held off the first waves of an assault, the bugs were crafty bastards. They adapted and changed into more formidable opponents. Lord knows what hell waited for us at lumber town.

As we hiked closer to the town, I doubted my decision to stay with Ronco. Even if my chances of survival on my own were zero, they were better than Ronco's. Dying of exposure in the forest was a better death than a bug one.

After we scaled the slope to the town and stood on its perimeter, everything was quiet. Ronco didn't say anything. He nodded to the others, and we all sat down. We waited for Bronco to arrive.

During the day, the place didn't look bad. It resembled your average American run-down town. Nothing about the place gave it away as a place of slaughter. Its white buildings weathered from time stood as silent guardians, like teeth lining a skull. Recalling my bravado the last time I rolled into town, I prepared for the worst.

After holding in my pee for a few hours, we saw movement on the other side of town. All of us remained still. Avoiding needless self-sacrifice required not running into a pack of man-eating bugs like a jackass.

When the large round figures of the Duffer clan appeared, we all sighed. I almost peed my pants. While Ronco and his men went to see Bronco, I went to a tree and relieved myself.

After I'd zipped up and returned to the Duffer gathering in the center of town, Bronco said, "Who the hell is this pipsqueak?"

I said, "I'm a friend of Ronco's."

Ronco said, "Yeah, he was also looking for someone who disappeared around here."

Bronco said, "Well, I don't like him. This is supposed to be for the family."

Ronco said, "You just want to let him die?"

While they looked at each other, a sound came from behind one of the buildings. We all turned toward it and waited. A small figure came out of one of the alleyways. A child.

After seeing us, it scampered away. We followed. We looked down the alleyway, but nothing was there.

Ronco said, "This is creepy."

We walked down the alley. It led to a dead end with a fence. Bronco said, "What the hell?"

All of a sudden, bug children started jumping from the tops of the buildings. Antennae protruded from their heads. Their eyes were cold, dark ocelli.

Bronco shouted, "Crap, they're using children. The goddam devils!"

As the last of these words left his mouth, one man unloaded a barrage of bullets from his rifle. The others followed suit building into a crescendo of automatic gunfire, screams and bug appendages flying everywhere. I dropped to my knees and put my head into the dirt with my hands over my ears. I wasn't armed and still suffered post-traumatic stress.

When the gunfire stopped, I opened my eyes and looked around. The alleyway looked like the bottom tray of a bug zapper. Nothing but insect heads and limbs everywhere.

I stood up and said, "Wow, you guys cleaned up."

Bronco said, "Shut up."

After exiting the alley, we walked back into the town square. Ronco said, "There," and pointed to a schoolhouse. We walked to it.

Ascending the steps and opening the doors, Bronco peered in. He whispered, "What the hell?"

After Bronco opened the door further, we all looked in. There, in the schoolhouse, child bugs curled up next to cocoons. We walked in further. Bronco cocked his gun and said, "I know what I'm going to do."

The gunmen encircled the room. Before they took their next steps, I fled. Bug children or not, watching this was not an option.

As I stumbled down the school steps and landed face first in the dirt, gunfire erupted. I kept my head down and put my hands over my ears again.

This time, I trembled. If any pee was left in me, it made its way out. The cursed bugs. They took over everything. They corrupted your dreams, your memories; anything they put their little cerci on.

Here, they corrupted children and their schools of learning. They offered us one solution. A simple, barbaric one, originating from the end of the gun.

When the Duffers exited the school, they were sweaty and tired. They looked ready for a nap. I said, "Are we done here? Can we leave now?"

Ronco answered me, "Nope."

We walked towards the church. For the first time, they noticed the form hanging from the spire. Bronco said, "You see that Ronco?"

Ronco said, "Those are Sam's shoes."

This place was all about the bugs and shoes. Our shoes were our dog tags. Our final remains. I looked at my shoes. They weren't great but not that bad either.

Bronco told two of his guys to climb the roof and pull the remains down. One lifted the other onto the sloped roof of the first-floor overhang and then the other helped lift him up. Taking care not to slip off the roof, they walked one foot in front of the other at a slight angle. When they reached the spire, one of them poked Sam's remains with his rifle stock, which broke free from the spire and crumpled to the roof. Consumed by insects and exposed to the elements for months, the remains turned to dust from a single touch.

The men scooped up the remains and walked over to the eaves above us. After yelling for us to watch out, they dropped the bones, clothes and ash to the ground in front of us.

Besides the bones and gray matter, all that remained of Sam were a pair of blue jeans and green hiking shoes. Ronco put the bones and shoes in his pack while Bronco sifted through the pockets of the pants.

In one of the pockets, his hand located something. He grimaced as he tried to work it out of the pants. Giving it a hard tug, he pulled out a square stone.

It was the goddamn image. My mouth went dry. I swallowed hard.

In addition to murder, Sam added thief to his titles. I was sure he no longer cared.

Bronco said, "What the hell is this?"

No one answered. I played dumb. This was not a group that valued honesty.

Ronco said, "Give it here."

After Bronco threw it to him, he took a look at it, put it in his pocket and said, "I will look it up later."

Bronco said, "Well, that's that. We found what we came here for. Let's get the hell out of here. This place makes me sick."

As we headed out of town, I gave the place one last look. I remembered my last group of friends who came here. Funny thing about me, I always managed to find friends. The problem was they didn't last long.

Chapter 31

BUGS, BUGS, BUGS

Ronco's ATVs were north of town, in the opposite direction from where the investigator had parked his car. To get there required a hike.

The first day was free of bugs. Our hike was peaceful. Only hills and streams slowed us down.

On the night of the first day, Ronco studied the stone we'd found on Sam by surfing the internet on his phone. His phone's signal was strong enough for him to discover everything we had. Web pages revealed pictures of the image in Japan and sands in Antarctica.

He said, "Holy cow, these bugs are everywhere and taking over. It's the end of the goddamn world."

Ronco was someone I trusted. Unlike the others, he saw the truth of what we faced. He knew we were in the end times.

I said, "I dream about the bugs."

He said, "Dream?"

I said, "'She Who Shall Not Be Named' visits me. She speaks to me."

He said, "Okay, you know you sound like a crack pot right now."

I said, "I have seen the same things you have. But I have also seen her. She comes to me in dreams."

Ronco let out a long whistle.

I said, "Listen. She told me if I came to her, I would know peace."

He said, "Yeah, you would know peace all right. You would be dead. Man, you are just going crazy from all these bugs. You better get your head checked."

I didn't say anything. He might be right.

Ronco and I didn't talk much after that. Although he looked at me like I was crazy, I didn't mind. He was right. I was crazy.

On the second day, we came across a field with bushes. It was a weird sight. In the middle of the forest was a clearing of black perennials. They looked painful to step on. Their stems were black and firm. Falling down in this patch might prove fatal.

Bronco said, "Look there's some kind of pack."

In the middle of the bushes lay a backpack.

Bronco turned to me and said, "Here's your chance to earn your keep, Chump. Go get us that pack."

I shrugged. I needed to do something around here. I walked into the center of the patch, knelt down, picked up the pack, and opened it. There was nothing inside.

Holding it up for them to see, I said, "It's empty."

Just as I started walking back, the plants moved. They pushed themselves up from the ground. I laughed. It was so odd seeing a whole patch of bushes rise up. This place was madness.

Everyone looked at me. I wore a crazy smile in a crazy field.

The bushes stopped moving. While I looked down at them, they burst from the ground, throwing dirt all around me. From underneath their perennial stems appeared the hairy abdomens of spiders. Their bellies were huge, the size of watermelons.

Surrounded, I knew this was the end. My madness had met its match. In one last act of penitence, I held my arms out, shut my eyes and lifted my face to the heavens.

I said, "Take me."

A brush of wind breezed my face. My eyes opened in time to see the spiders flying across the field towards the Duffers. Ronco and Bronco saw them coming too and rolled down a hill, evading the bugs. The others were not so lucky. They stood there frozen in fear with stupid

166

looks on their faces as the spiders' perennial pedipalps pierced their heads and brains.

I stood alone in the clearing now empty of bushes. Across from me, I saw Ronco and Bronco staring at me in awe. I was unharmed. Not one bug touched me.

Bronco yelled, "You are a freak! A bug just like the others!"

Ronco and Bronco ran, leaving me alone. I watched the spiders feast on the dead and waited for them to eat me. Since it took them some time, I sat down. When their skittering stopped, I stood back up. They didn't come. They put their asses back in the ground.

This was not the end I hoped for. I was a mad freak. A saint to the bugs. Their first true believer. I was a prophet for the end of the world, even though I didn't know what to say.

I walked in the direction from where Ronco and Bronco ran. Hopefully, it was the right way out of here. They never did give me a compass.

I didn't run. I no longer feared the bugs. If watermelon-sized spiders didn't want me, I doubted any of the other insects desired me. I was the safest animal in the forest.

The forest was a great place to find myself. Except for the wind in the trees, it was quiet. Its air was fresh and fragrant. The forest lacked the pressures of normal life. No bosses or fraternity members or teachers harassed me here.

I hiked to a valley. On the opposite side, hauling ass up a slope, was Ronco and Bronco. They looked scared as hell, scrambling up the hill and yelling at each other. Were they scared of me or the spiders?

I kept walking. Isn't that what the evil pursuers do? Walk?

As I descended into the valley, I lost sight of the Duffers. Next to a stream lay some of their belongings. Why they left them was a mystery. I noticed some rifle rounds in a tree. Were they killing trees now?

Going up the hill, I found one of their shoes. Those idiots. Shoes were valuable here. They were the only way to identify the body.

Further up, I found some pants. They were covered in blood. In one of the pockets was a wallet. Pulling it out and flipping through it, I found Bronco's identification and thousands of dollars. I suspected he was a thief, stealing from the bodies he found in the Smokies. Believing Bronco worked a good paying job was a joke.

At the top of the hillside, Bronco sat against a tree. Well, part of him sat there. His shoulders and head were all that remained.

I said, "Man, you don't look good."

He responded, "Ugh, agh, help."

I jumped out of my shoes. How the hell was he still alive! There wasn't enough blood in his body to make his heart beat or enough lungs left for him to breathe. He was a tough dude and a blabbermouth. When my time came, I promised to go quiet.

I waited for him to say something else, but he didn't. I moved on, going straight into the woods. On a tree stump lay human organs. Leaving leftovers meant the bugs were full. I expected to find a group of fat bugs next.

In a small clearing lined with fallen trees, I found Ronco. He was in better shape than Bronco. About half of him remained. The bugs looked full and bored, crawling slowly over Ronco and nibbling at his flesh.

I said, "Ronco?"

He said, "You have to do it."

I said, "Do what?"

He said, "Kill their leader. The one you told me about."

I said, "How?"

He said, "I don't know. But they don't eat you. Find their leader and end her."

I said, "Okay, I guess."

Ronco closed his eyes and lay his head to the side.

I said, "Hey, are you still alive?"

He didn't say anything. He was a goner. Reduced to a piece of meat on the ground, Ronco's body had seen better days. Seeing him this way forced me to remember how he looked before. When he was whole, he was full of power and confidence. With his body eaten, he looked like meat on a sandwich.

I said, "I'm sorry, Ronco. I will kill her for you."

Chapter 32

ESCAPE FROM SMOKY MOUNTAIN

After finding Ronco's keys on the ground, I set out to find the ATVs. To my surprise, they were less than a hundred yards away. Ronco was close. The poor bastard might have lived if he was a little faster.

After pressing the starter a few times, the ATV fired up. Instead of heading out, I turned the handlebars and went back into the forest. The private investigator's car remained in the parking lot on the other side. Since I didn't know any other way out of this place, it would be my best way home.

The sun shone high in the sky. Still plenty of hours in the day for the Mud Caves. Finding the keys among the rocks and body parts presented a problem, but one I felt good about solving. My luck in discovering all sorts of shoes, pants, keys and wallets up to this point boosted my confidence in finding dick's keys as well.

Riding the ATV was fun until I remembered my last time here. Focusing on my handling of the ATV over the rough terrain distracted me from thinking about my past. Keeping my mind on the present kept it from going to dark places.

At the Mud Caves, I turned off my ATV and dismounted. I took a few steps, and a glint caught my eye. Neatly placed on a rock were the keys. I stopped. Was *she* reading my mind now? Or by some bizarre chance did they land there after the investigator exploded?

I picked up the keys and examined them. Not a scratch on them. The power of the blast blew them to safety. I jingled them in my hand and put them in my pocket. Today was my lucky day after all.

As I drove away, the feeling of someone watching my every move hovered over me. It reminded me of my mother watching me when I was young. It wanted me to know it was there.

Pressing my foot down on the ATV's accelerator, I hauled ass. No more hanging around this godforsaken place. I was on a mission. Limiting the amount of time I spent in this goddamn forest required riding as fast and far as I could in the next few hours.

Driving into the night, I stopped the ATV only when I almost hit a tree. After turning off the cycle and getting off, I propped myself up against it and tried catching some sleep before I left at daybreak.

I dreamed of her.

Holding my tiny body up against a cold dark sky in one hand, she said, "Finally, you are here. I have waited so long. So long!"

Throwing me up in the air, she opened her mandibles and I fell into her mouth. Thorns on the side of her throat shredded my skin as I fell towards her stomach. The pain was excruciating.

I screamed, "Help me! I'm lost!"

She cooed, "Hush now, child. It's not that bad."

When I awoke in the cold dark, my skin was on fire. My body hurt like someone scratched me all over.

The forest was quiet. Not a soul around, or so they wanted me to believe. The bugs obliterated every living thing in the forest. I was the only one who they let live.

The quiet hit me. No buzzing. After coming here, I no longer experienced buzzing fits. Even when bugs rose from the ground and impaled my allies, my mind was calm. This was not welcome news for me. The only thing which found peace around the bugs was a bug.

I didn't sleep anymore that evening. I stared straight ahead and waited for the night to release me from this hell. I had a date with a real bitch.

The moment the sun's rays flashed across the horizon, I jumped on the ATV and fired it up. Screw this place. Time to head home after another slaughter.

Imagining her spying on me from above like a drone, I hoped "She Who Shall Not Be Named" saw me. With a sore ass, tired arms, and a list of dead friends longer than most family trees, I felt like crap. I'm sure my appearance wasn't much better.

I looked forward to going home. Los Angeles offered me a respite. A rest before my last great adventure.

Chapter 33

MY LAST GREAT ADVENTURE

My expedition required transportation, lodging and clothing. With my savings and Bronco's loot, I had enough money to make it happen.

Planning was everything. Knowing the right clothes to wear was a matter of life and death. Securing a ship reservation in advance took four months' notice. And a trustworthy guide was a rare commodity.

My resources were all on the internet. Researching things was easy. Planning your final journey on a keyboard was a miracle of the modern age.

I told my house brothers of my intent to move out at the end of summer. In reality, I planned on leaving the material plane before then.

On the walls of our house, group pictures of all our former brothers hung in silence. With their smiles and drunk expressions, they looked down at us with mute joy. As a member of the last class, I hated my role in the end of this. The end of all joy in our house and the world.

My last meeting with Suzie unearthed painful feelings. Emotions of loss and love topped the list. Suzie was the last shining star of my life. She wasn't my lover, just someone who cared.

Once I told her my plans, she said, "Wow, bring me back a snowball. And if you meet the abominable snowman, tell him I said hello!"

Most of our co-workers believed she didn't take me seriously, but she did. Suzie and I were similar people. We were both "opposites." We both acted the opposite of what we felt. We cared for people but didn't want to show it.

Not that it mattered but I donated most of my stuff to Goodwill. Removing my stuff from the house relieved my brothers of the burden. And it might bring comfort to someone else's last days.

My last meal in Los Angeles was Mexican. A place down by the beach served good tacos and offered great sunsets. Sitting outside on one of their plastic benches, the ocean breeze ruffled my hair, and the last rays of the setting sun blinded me.

Time, I headed out of town. By now, John's father knew the private investigator was missing. This whole time he was waiting for us to return with some news of his son. I regret not telling him the truth, but I now had a purpose to my life. Getting held up by an angry dad was not an option.

As my plane took off for Chile, this was my last image of Los Angeles. LA waved goodbye to me.

Chapter 34

ANTARCTICA

Through my university, I signed up for a visit to a research station in Antarctica. In case hiking further south was necessary, I hired a guide from Chile. When my plane landed, he met me at the airport.

He greeted me holding a sign and took me to a hotel. We drank coffee at a cafe in the hotel and then I went to my room. Since our ship didn't leave for a few days, there was plenty of time for me to tour the city, but I didn't care to. The world was ending.

My guide's name was Vicente. He grew up in San Pedro de Atacama and worked with contractors setting up biological research stations in Antarctica. He was between jobs when I hired him.

In the cafe, he told me some recent stories about Antarctica. He said that midge insects were growing in number and size. Since climate change threatened the midge with extinction, these findings baffled researchers.

More alarming, he said there was an increase in missing people and ships. Until recently, ships crashed into rocks every five years. Over the past two weeks, the seas and snow claimed ships and people every day.

Bringing Vicente into this was amoral but saving the world required it. Finding "She Who Shall Not Be Named" demanded his help. Becoming lost and dying in the cold wastes without completing my mission was pointless.

In my prior emails with Vicente, I told him I was an entomologist with expertise in setting up expeditions in North Carolina and New Mexico. And I needed to scout Antarctica for a future expedition.

I was lucky that midge insects were growing in Antarctica. This was probably why Vicente took my story at face value and didn't ask me questions.

For our trip, I packed waterproof pants, jackets and boots as well as wag bags and water filters. Our phones were useless there. We packed enough food for a week, but my journey would take less time. Vicente was unaware my trip was one way.

The morning of our embarkation, Vicente picked me up at the hotel. A consummate professional, he bought snacks and canned coffee. Our ride to the docks took five minutes, which was enough for me to power down my food.

Walking up the narrow gangplank with chain link handholds, I looked at the frigid waters beneath my feet. Although Antarctica was a frozen hell, it lacked the power to hold Satan. I wished I could make it colder.

A fear gripped me. If I became frozen here and reawakened a hundred years later, my life would suck. The bugs would own everything. The future was not very bright.

She'd taken my hopes and dreams from me. She'd taunted me with promises of peace, the one thing I could never have. She was cruel and her cruelty lacked any purpose beyond pain. Whatever cold void spawned her before the beginning of time proved the dominant hand of the universe. The blackness of space allowing the existence of earth for a fleeting, forgettable moment in its history was its only miracle.

Once on board the ship, we went straight to our cabin. Our cabin faced the rear of the vessel. It was quiet and offered a broad view of the ice ocean. The only bad part was we felt every movement of the ship. Good thing I didn't get sea sick.

The cabin itself was small with one porthole and a tiny sitting area. The two single beds provided adequate rest for our voyage.

Neither Vicente nor I talked much. For him, our voyage was work. For me, it was the end of the line.

Later that day, we ate lunch at the mess hall. Besides the crew, we were the only ones onboard. The captain wore a worried, angry expression. Everyone seemed to sense the world wasn't right, but I was the only one who knew why.

That night, she didn't visit me because I didn't dream. She didn't need to. She'd hijacked my life. Lord knows what her true plans were – or what she'd made me.

The sound of screaming men and the jolt of my body falling on the floor woke me. Vicente and I looked out our cabin window. The ship was on the rocks.

Welcome to Antarctica.

Chapter 36

END OF THE LINE

When Vicente and I walked on deck, we saw bodies of sailors. Midges the size of a fist skittered across the deck, darting from one body to the next. Insect swarms which looked like small tornados whirled around the bow.

The moment Vicente took two steps onto the deck, the tornadoes darted towards him. The bugs impaled him. Their impact sounded like hard slaps. The slapping continued for several minutes until his body broke down into a mound of flesh on the deck.

At first, I hid behind a bulkhead. My worry about losing my guide turned to worry about getting off the ship. Bringing poor little Vicente here was a mistake. Coming here was bad for everyone.

Collecting myself, I remembered why I came here. It was the end of life on earth. The time for me to stand tall was now.

I went below deck and started looking in the cargo hold. I found dynamite used for surveys and glaciers. I lined my jacket and pants with them along with blasting caps. I was the first snow man suicide bomber.

After stepping back on deck, I went to the side of the boat and surveyed the terrain. I didn't see anything. I shouted, "How the hell am I supposed to find you, you stupid bitch!"

When I turned back around to look for the gangplank, I faced two swarms of bugs hovering in front of me. As I moved to go between them, they swarmed me. Bugs went inside my ears, nose and mouth. They impaled my arms and legs.

They didn't destroy me. They possessed my body instead. They threw me into the ice water and made me swim to shore. Standing up,

I was in agony. Although the ice water killed a few of the bugs, it froze my extremities while most of the bugs burrowed further into my body.

With my head down, they forced me to walk. The flesh on my hands sagged and turned gray. I was a rotter.

I walked for hours in the cold. I felt sleepy as the early stages of hypothermia set in. Thinking myself dead before she could tell me what a dumb ass I was, the bugs lifted my head up and before me she stood.

"She Who Shall Not Be Named," was just like my dreams. She stood more than a hundred meters tall on a ground of sand and snow. On either side of her were two large, winged bugs a mere twenty meters tall. Out of their wings spewed hundreds of thousands of flying insects. They chanted as their swarm blacked out the sky.

She giggled. "Silly one. Why do you make it so hard? Your kind are like little ants infesting the world. You eat and tear down everything, making the planet sick. It's not all your fault though. You were born with these little holes in you. You try to fill it with friends, love, adventure and parties. But it's never enough, is it?"

I didn't say anything. I'd vowed to myself I wouldn't die a blabbermouth like Bronco.

She said, 'Like everyone I have eaten before, you don't need to search anymore. I will make you whole. You will become one with the universe."

The joke was on her. I still wore my suicide jacket. Once it touched those thorns in her throat, we would share the same fate.

She lifted one of her gargantuan legs and stepped on me. The explosion caused my remaining head and torso to spin across the ice. It was one hell of a ride.

As I looked at her with tired weary eyes, she picked up my remains and flicked me into her mouth like a hors d'oeuvre.

As my body traveled down her throat, I noticed two things. First, there were no thorns. And two, I felt free.

I saw across all universes in every moment of infinite time. She existed in all dimensions drawing a dark outline in a black sky everywhere she exhibited a physical form. It was impossible to name her because she was everything, everywhere, all at once.

Through her, I was one with the universe. I said, "Thank you."